# THE SHEIKH'S REVENGE BY SEDUCTION

DIANA FRASER

**The Sheikh's Revenge by Seduction**

by Diana Fraser



ISBN 978-0-9951447-9-8 (epub)
ISBN 978-0-9951410-5-6 (print)

*A sheikh intent on revenge, a Englishwoman caught in a trap, a love that cannot be denied...*

**—Secrets of the Sheikhs—**

The Sheikh's Revenge by Seduction
The Sheikh's Secret Love Child
The Sheikh's Marriage Trap

**—The Sheikhs of Havilah—**

The Sheikh's Secret Baby
Bought by the Sheikh
The Sheikh's Forbidden Lover
Surrender to the Sheikh

**—Desert Kings—**

Wanted: A Wife for the Sheikh
The Sheikh's Bargain Bride
The Sheikh's Lost Lover
Awakened by the Sheikh
Claimed by the Sheikh
Wanted: A Baby by the Sheikh

For more information about this author, visit:
https://www.dianafraser.net

# PROLOGUE

Sheikh Rayan ibn Mohammed Aziz burst through the double doors of the palace's meeting room and strode over to his two half-brothers—Sheikh Zeeshan, King of Ahmar, and Sheikh Adam, the youngest of the three.

"Is it true?" Rayan said between gritted teeth, trying to contain the grief and anger which roiled just under the surface. "Is Madaniya dead?" His voice only trembled slightly as he spoke his half-sister's name.

Zeeshan stopped pacing and looked up at Rayan with a grief-stricken expression, which Rayan would never allow to show on his own face. Zeeshan nodded and looked away.

Adam stepped forward and put his hand on Zeeshan's shoulder in a gesture of solidarity. He looked at Rayan with his usual direct glare.

"Yes," Adam said. "It's true. Her maid found her."

"Was she..." Rayan swallowed. "Is anyone else implicated?"

Zeeshan shook his head again as he slumped into a chair and put his head in his hands. "No, no one. She died by her own hand."

Rayan turned away from the sight of his eldest half-brother almost destroyed by the news that their beautiful sister—so bright and fun-loving—was no longer alive.

"Why? Why would she do this? Didn't she say anything to anyone to explain this? Not a word to any of us?"

"She told me," Zeeshan said dully, "that she was about to marry the man she'd been seeing."

"Who?"

"An English aristocrat by the name of Charles le Harivel. He was entirely unsuitable for her—much older, a playboy." He shook his head. "I told her she was being foolish and she should reconsider. But she said that there was nothing to reconsider, and that, besides, she was pregnant and so marriage was inevitable."

"Pregnant?" Rayan gasped. "Madaniya was pregnant?" He couldn't believe that his half-sister had been so foolish as to have unprotected sex.

"Yes. She claimed she loved him," Zeeshan said with a deep sigh. He shook his head. "She claimed they were to marry."

"And so… what happened?"

Adam tossed his phone to Rayan, who read the message—the last message from his sister. He scanned it and then re-read it, and in a heartbeat his grief turned to anger. He passed the phone back to Adam.

"He refused to marry her," Zeeshan said. "*That* man refused to marry my sister and went off with someone else instead."

"Bastard!" said Adam between gritted teeth.

Rayan clamped his mouth shut. 'Bastard' didn't go anywhere near to what he thought of this man.

"Where is he now?"

"Charles le Harivel is currently sunning himself in the Caribbean with some young American blonde."

Rayan gave a tight nod. "Right."

The harsh sun shone into the room, illuminating the three brothers' grief-stricken faces—three different men, one unavoidable conclusion.

Zeeshan's face hardened. "Our culture demands vengeance on this man who destroyed our most beloved sister."

"An eye for an eye..." said Adam.

"And a tooth for a tooth," finished Rayan. "And we will avenge our sister's death in the time-honored way. What do we know about this man?"

"He's an English aristocrat with a large estate," said Adam. "He's extremely wealthy and he gets through women like water. Our sister didn't stand a chance with him."

"The question is how to avenge our sister? We need to identify this man's weakness," said Zeeshan.

"Does he have family?" Rayan asked.

"One daughter," Adam replied.

"Is she married?"

"No," said Adam. "She appears to be single and living on the le Harivel estate in England. Her name is Lauren Alexandra le Harivel and she's his only living child. It appears that she runs his estate and companies. Without her, he wouldn't have any of his wealth or what little reputation he has." He leaned heavily onto the table. "Apparently she's the apple of his eye."

"How do you know all this?"

"The moment I heard about Madaniya, I began researching everything we need to know about the man." Adam flung a bundle of papers onto the table. "She's his weak link. She's his Achilles heel. It's through her we can avenge Madaniya's death."

Rayan twisted the papers around so he could see the

photo of the woman. He frowned. “She’s plain—I wouldn’t look twice at her. Why is she the apple of his eye?”

“She’s the last of the le Harivel line stretching back to the Norman Conquest, when the family were given the lands they still own. Whatever she looks like, not only is this woman running his empire, but she shares his name and his blood. The bloodline means everything to him. That, my brothers, is how we will get to him.”

“Seduce and discard, just as this woman’s father did to our beloved sister.” For a moment, Zeeshan’s expression teetered on the cusp of indecision. Rayan put his hand on his brother, who he knew housed a softer heart than either him or Adam.

“It must be done. You know there is no other way.”

“Rayan’s right,” said Adam.

All three pairs of eyes were trained on the grainy image of a woman’s pensive face, framed by a hat which appeared too large, and her father who appeared too domineering. The face itself told them nothing. It could have been drawn by a child. Indeterminate features, nervous eyes, a half-smile that appeared to expect nothing—which was good because nothing would be what she’d get.

“I’ll do it,” Rayan said quietly. “I’ve nothing to lose and more anger than the two of you put together. Besides, Zeeshan, you have the country to run. You cannot be seen to be embroiled in this. Let me do it. I’d consider it an honor.”

He knew he had them; he knew they couldn’t contradict him. They understood each other well and respected each other for their distinct personalities. Neither of his brothers could deny that he was the most suitable person for the job. He twisted the papers around again so he could read the woman’s name, rolled them up and tapped them on the table. He’d absorbed one piece of information only—her name. It was all he needed to focus his hatred on. He'd read up on the rest later.

"Leave it to me."

He thrust the papers into his pocket and walked away. He didn't need a second look at the papers. The name he'd focus his hate and anger on would burn in his mind forever.

Lauren Alexandra le Harivel wouldn't know what had hit her.

# CHAPTER 1

*Two weeks later...*

"Fun in the sun," Lauren Alexandra le Harivel read in the online gossip blog. The photo accompanying the blog showed her father—tanned and handsome with his thick gray hair and piercing blue eyes—and his latest conquest. This one was blonde, but otherwise in the same mode—tall, skinny, with unrealistically large breasts and lips that pouted without the woman having to bother to move a muscle—if she could. Lauren sometimes wondered if her father would have been able to tell his girlfriends apart in a line-up.

She snapped the laptop closed and tried not to let the familiar feelings of rejection swamp her. He hadn't been with her on her birthday for years, so why should she think this year would be any different?

She tapped the shiny metal of the laptop with increased agitation. How could he treat her this way? He claimed she meant more to him than anything, and she'd always believed him, despite the lack of his actions backing up his words.

But, with every passing year, her trust in his love had been chipped away. At first she'd been distressed, then sad, and now? She glanced out the window, her eyes momentarily blinded by the bright morning sunshine which had risen above the row of lime trees which lined the drive. And now, she felt nothing but anger—anger at always coming at the bottom of her father's list of priorities.

If *he* wouldn't put her first, then she must. Starting today.

She rose from the mahogany desk and looked out the tall window of the second-floor sitting room in which she did most of her work. She preferred the seclusion of the sitting room to her father's library. It was quieter here, and she could manage the estate more effectively with her laptop than she could in person. Her staff didn't dwarf her, and her quiet voice could be heard more effectively through written communication.

And she also had the advantage of being able to see anyone entering or leaving the estate, as well as the courtyard and stables. It was her vantage point. But this morning, rather than checking out whether the deliveries had arrived for the estate farm, her gaze was once more directed to the stable yard. She soon saw who she was looking for.

Tall, dark, and powerfully built, the estate's newest employee was hard at work shaping a horse shoe. Despite the early hour, the sun was high in the sky, promising yet another brilliant summer's day. Clearly it was already hot in the stable yard as the man had stripped off his shirt, revealing dark skin and muscles the likes of which Lauren had never seen before. None of the other workers were built like him and none, for sure, made her feel so compelled to stand and gaze at him. As he swung the hammer back and forth, the sun caught the gleam of sweat on his pumped-up muscles. The rhythmic ding of the iron shoe as it hit the anvil echoed around the cobbled stable yard. There was a strength in his actions, and a savagery about his movements, which heightened her primitive reaction to the sight of his bare back.

And, if that weren't enough, when he came close to the horse he changed. From aggressive and strong, his touch gentled while still being firm. Lauren's skin prickled as she watched his hand sweep down the horse's leg with a reassurance which meant the flighty Arab was instantly calmed. For some reason it made the breath in Lauren's throat catch and hold until he'd finished fixing the racehorse's shoe to her hoof.

When he released the horse's hoof back onto the cobbled ground, he swept his hand over the horse's hindquarters and Lauren felt a corresponding shimmer of arousal at the sight. She swallowed, clutched at the heavy velvet curtains and kneeled weakly on the chintz-covered window seat, her eyes still fixed on the man. Then the man inclined his head to the horse as if he were talking to her, gave her another a gentle pat and led the horse away, disappearing from view behind the corner of the stables.

Lauren was suddenly aware of how long she'd been standing staring at the man and guiltily looked around, reassured that she hadn't been observed. Not that anyone paid her much attention, anyway. She stepped away from the window, took a deep breath, and sat back at her desk. But the laptop's screensaver continued to swirl over her screen. The papers in her in-tray remained undisturbed and the ding of her phone went unanswered. Her thoughts lingered on the man.

He'd arrived only a week ago. She hadn't hired him. She left that sort of thing to her estate manager, but she'd seen his ability with horses, and she'd noticed him from the very first moment he'd arrived. He would have been hard to miss. Tall, broad, muscled and dark, his air was commanding in a way which had made her question the estate manager. He didn't look like the average stable-hand, didn't hold himself with the usual sullen, obsequious manner of one of the estate hands. But the manager had assured her he was nobody of significance—just a traveler who had amazing instincts with horses. After seeing how he'd handled the crazy Arab stallion they'd bought at enormous expense, the manager had hired him on the spot.

And Lauren's gaze had been hooked and captivated by the stranger every day since his arrival. Despite her discreet checks, all that was known of him was his name and his ability with horses.

"Rayan," she whispered to herself. It was a name as mysterious as the man himself.

She should stay and work, but after reluctantly acknowledging to herself how unlikely that it was that her father would turn up for her birthday next week, she didn't feel like working. What she felt like was being reckless, striking out—doing something for herself, *only* for herself. What she felt like was indulging her curiosity about the mysterious stranger with the exotic name, a gentle touch and a barely concealed primitive strength. There was something intoxicating about him, something she did not know how to describe, or how to rationalize. She only knew she wanted to get closer to him.

She snapped shut the laptop. She was no use here. No, she'd find out a little more about this Rayan, and then she'd return to work. After all, it was essential for every employer to know about her employees, wasn't it?

She rose from the desk, picked up her sensible cardigan to hide the camisole she considered to be too revealing to wear outside the house, and walked to the door. She paused, glanced at the window, and tossed the cardigan onto a sofa. She preferred to wear discreet clothes, clothes which covered her bare skin. After all, it wouldn't be seemly for the lady of the manor to walk around in the kind of clothes her father preferred his girlfriends to wear. But today, the sky was a brilliant blue and the sun's rays which shone across the heirloom rug were bright. It was going to be a hot day. And, after such a long, cool winter and spring, Lauren was drawn to heat like a moth to a flame. She just hoped she wouldn't burn.

RAYAN'S NECK PRICKLED, and he glanced up at the ivy-clad manor house. He thought he saw a movement at one of the second-floor windows, but it was gone before he could double-check. Maybe he'd imagined it. Maybe it was simply the warmth of the summer sunshine on his back. He'd forgotten how warm English summers could be. The temperatures were nowhere close to the unrelenting heat of the Ahmar desert, but warm enough to build up a sweat. Especially when shoeing a fine Arab mare, such as this one.

He rubbed the horse's flank, settling it as it nickered, as if sensing someone from her own part of the world. He took hold of the reins and walked the horse back to the stable. Only when she was comfortable did he leave the stable, sliding the bolt behind him. Through the top of the stable door, the mare poked out her head as if reluctant to break the connection. Rayan smiled and rubbed the horse's nose, muttering to her in Arabic—words of endearment, words of love, which he only ever uttered to animals. Animals never betrayed him. Providing you treated them right, you could rely on the love of an animal.

Suddenly the horse's ears twitched and her eyes shot to one side. Rayan didn't turn immediately, although he, like the horse, could sense they were being watched. Instead, he took a few moments to calm the mare before turning slowly to find a girl, the sun behind her obscuring her features, standing at the entrance to the stable yard, looking at him. Disappointment filled him. He'd been hoping to see the lady of the manor, the high and mighty Lauren le Harivel. But he'd been here a week and hadn't yet caught sight of her.

He was about to return to his duties when the girl walked over to him. She was short, slender and wore jeans and a camisole top which revealed pale shoulders and a distinct lack of bust. His gaze rested for a few moments on the coral necklace she wore. It stirred memories of a different coral necklace, a different country, and the love of someone who he hadn't appreciated at the time.

Lazily, he allowed his gaze to move over her hair—which was blonde but scraped back into a severe and very long ponytail—before he met her gaze. Her eyes were very blue, very knowing. They were eyes that definitely belonged to an adult woman, not a girl. He stood stock still. It *was* her. And yet she looked different to her photos.

As she approached, he saw she wore no make-up on her pale face. But what was striking was her manner and air of authority, which was reflected only in her eyes. She extended her hand to him and introduced herself with a voice which was low and husky, and totally at odds with her mousy appearance.

"Hello, I don't think we've met. I'm Lauren le Harivel."

He was suddenly conscious that he was only wearing a pair of old jeans, and his hands were dirty with horse grease and grime. He gritted his teeth. If she wanted to shake hands with her staff, then so be it. Without wiping his hand on his jeans, he took hold of her hand in a firm grip. She looked surprised as his hand engulfed hers in a manner that held no subservience in it.

"Rayan," he said.

"Yes." She smiled, and her face immediately became

anything but ordinary. It lit up, revealing perfect white teeth and a smile that brightened and settled in her eyes. "I know. I've heard about your skills with our horses." She appeared to be staring fixedly into his eyes, as if she was scared to look anywhere else.

"I was raised with horses."

"Really?" she said, in that clipped English way which he hadn't heard for so long.

"Yes." He didn't elaborate. He wasn't here to tell this woman his life story. Not unless he had to, that was. And, by the way her pale cheeks had flushed with pink as her eyes had strayed to his bare chest, he suspected he wouldn't have to supply too many details about his own life. He took a measured step closer, and her blue eyes darkened.

She tried to withdraw her hand, but he held it firmer for one long second before allowing her to release it, a hint to her that, no matter her pedigree or wealth, it was *he* who would hold the power between them. She placed her palm against her jeans, as if trying to control it. For the first time since he'd decided on his fate, he thought this might just turn out to be fun.

"Well, that's good then. We certainly could do with your, er, skills around here."

He didn't reply.

"So, er, are you settling in all right?"

He folded his arms. "Yes."

"Right." She nodded over-enthusiastically, as if making up for his lack of response. "So, there's nothing you need?"

"No."

She smiled, but the smile faded and she looked around as if unsure. For a woman who ran the entire le Harivel estate, and who was, apparently, the most adored daughter of her father, she didn't appear very sure of herself with the opposite sex. He cleared his throat. It looked like he'd have to talk to the woman—something he wasn't known for—otherwise she'd leave, and he might not have another opportunity like this. After all, he'd been here a week already and had only caught glimpses of her.

"There is something," he said.

She stopped mid-turn and looked up at him with a surprised expression. "And what's that?"

"The accommodation," he said. It was all he could think of to keep her with him, alone, where he could begin the charm offensive his brothers had teased him about. He wasn't known for his charm.

"You've been given the rooms above the stables, haven't you?"

"That's right."

"What's the matter with them?"

"Come with me, and I'll show you." She looked hesitant. "It's best seen."

"Oh." She shrugged and glanced at her watch. "Okay. I have some time until my next appointment."

Good, he thought. He just hoped he'd be able to invent some reason to take her to his rooms before they got there. He stepped aside and indicated she should precede him. She climbed the wooden stairs which ran up the side of the stables, and he followed. Her behind might be small, but it was shapely, he'd give her that. Her appearance was deceptive. Her features and figure were neat, nothing out of the ordinary, and she made no attempt to draw attention to either. But there was a light behind her eyes, and an energy in her movements which suggested there was more to her than met the eye. He was intrigued.

She stood on the small deck outside the door, waiting for him to enter. He opened the door and stood aside.

He followed her inside and cast a quick glance around, searching for an excuse to detain her. His eyes alighted on radiators. He pointed to them. "The heaters are controlled centrally. It's too hot up here." It was, but it didn't bother him.

"Oh!" She frowned and looked from the radiator back at him. She bent down and checked the valve on the radiator. He was rewarded with a view of her pert rear. He had a sudden and vivid vision of how it would feel if he were pressed up against her. She gave a small grunt as she tried to shift the valve, but it was stuck hard. And so was he. He picked up his shirt from the back of the couch to hide the evidence.

She stood up and grimaced. "Looks like you're right. I'll have our electrician look into it. I'm sure he should be able to put it onto another circuit, or something. But…"

He cocked his head to one side. She blushed prettily. "But what?" he prompted.

She shrugged and smiled, endearingly unsure. "I'd have thought you'd be used to the heat coming from… where was it?"

She was fishing for information. He'd given the bare minimum to the manager who'd employed him. But he wanted to get her onside, he wanted this relationship to become a lot more than employee–employer. "I've been traveling all around. Mainly the Persian Gulf area."

"Whereabouts?"

It was too soon. He needed to forge a connection with her before he told her anything more about himself.

He allowed a slow smile to slide across his face. "A small town in a small country. You wouldn't know it." He reached out and touched her arm. Her frown disappeared. She lifted her face to his, her lips apart, and her eyes wide and trusting. Another soft blush bloomed on her cheeks. "Would you like a drink?" he asked. "A coffee perhaps?" He nodded to the dallah. "I could make you some genuine Arab coffee."

She grimaced, biting her lip as if torn. He needed her to stay.

"It's an excuse," he added, deciding that, out of all his options, honesty would be the most persuasive with this woman. He liked the way her blush deepened.

"I'd like to talk a little about your stable of Arabs," he added. He would only take honesty so far. "I think there are improvements that could be made to their stabling, and their feed."

Her relief was palpable and endearing. He had to swallow a smile.

"Of course," she said, in that seductive voice of hers. "Yes, please, a coffee would be lovely."

He smiled to himself as he left her to take a seat while he went to the kitchenette and prepared the coffee. This woman needed to be lulled into a false sense of security in order to spend time with him. She was attracted to him, that much was clear. But it seemed she wasn't accustomed to surrendering to her sexual urges. Looked like she'd need a little help, help he was willing to give.

She looked up as he brought the dallah and cups over and placed them on the small, three-legged coffee table.

"It's like Turkish coffee, which you may have tasted."

She shook her head, and her ponytail swung, reinforcing the girlish look. She'd taken a seat in one of the two easy chairs, separated by the table. He sat opposite her and poured two coffees. She looked at him with an embarrassed frown and then turned away once more, as if scared to meet his gaze.

"No, I haven't tasted Turkish coffee before. Or," she said, swilling the thick, dark liquid in the small cup, "anything like this. I haven't traveled far."

He frowned and focused on his coffee. How could a

young woman, so wealthy, with so many advantages, not have traveled?

"I've been busy here, on the estate," she said by way of explanation.

"Of course." He watched her take a sip and was irrationally pleased to see the ripple of emotions flow over her face. First there was pleasure at the consistency on her tongue. This was followed by shock at the intense taste, then surprise as her taste buds and senses were stimulated like no amount of instant coffee—which appeared to be the drink of choice for the staff on the estate—could do.

"It's good," she said with a smile. "Very different to the instant coffee I drink, but very good."

"The instant coffee you drink isn't coffee. This"—he indicated the small cup before him—"is real coffee. In fact the word 'coffee' comes from the Arabic *qahwa*."

"*Qahwa*", she repeated. The word sounded awkward on her tongue. "How do you spell it?"

He shook his head. "It's best to listen to the word rather than think about how it is spelled. *Qahwa*," he said, correcting her pronunciation.

"*Qahwa*," she repeated with more confidence this time.

"We usually prepare it with cardamom, but sugar can also be added."

"But this time you've shown me it unadulterated by any other taste."

He nodded. He'd done it on purpose.

"I like it." She smiled and then the smile became more uncertain, as if she wasn't sure she should continue. But she did. "I'd like to try it with cardamom some time, too."

He smiled and nodded. He'd got her. All he had to do now was reel her in. "It would be my pleasure." And he was beginning to think it would be.

Their gazes met and tangled for a delicious moment before she looked away with an air of surprise.

"Is there something the matter?" he asked.

She looked back at him, her face flickering with confusion.

"No. I'm just finding it strange, talking to someone like you."

"How do you mean?"

"I mean someone who isn't English. You seem so 'other', for want of a better word. And yet you speak flawless English. It's a strange combination."

He took a sip of his coffee, set it down on the table, buying time to decide how much to tell her. He looked up into her innocent, trusting eyes and realized he'd have to tell her more than he'd expected if he wanted to lower her guard.

"Although I spent my early years in the Middle East, I lived for many years in England with my mother. After her death I returned to my father's country." He waited to see if she'd ask him to name the country. He still hadn't decided if he'd tell her or not. Would she ask?

She held his gaze steadily. "And where is this country?"

"Ahmar." He watched her carefully but, apart from a small frown, she didn't appear to register any recognition. Maybe her father hadn't shared with her the nationality of his ex-lover.

"And did you feel 'other' there, too?"

"For a time, I did." He was surprised at her ability to put herself in his shoes. What could this woman know about feeling a stranger amongst his own people? He remembered the pain of trying to shed his Englishness, of trying to fit in. "But not now. However, in England I was, am, and always will be, a foreigner."

She sat back and rested against the back of her chair, as if she'd received an explanation which satisfied her. "It must be strange for you, being caught between two worlds."

He shrugged. "No. It's simply how others see me." He leaned forward, resting his arms on his thighs, spearing her gaze with his own. She stilled. "I know who I am. I am an Ahmari, through and through. I think like one, I act like one, I *am* one. No amount of perfect English will change that. But, I'm curious. Why is it you understand this sense of 'otherness' of which you speak, Miss le Harivel?"

"Please, call me Lauren."

His eyebrow shot up in surprise. For someone so wealthy and so powerful, she was surprisingly informal. It wouldn't happen in his country. He wondered how informal she could be. He leaned forward further, bringing his head closer to hers. Her eyes flared with awareness and then tightened under a small smile. The smile held.

"Lauren." He tested the word on his tongue and found he liked it. He also liked her response.

He was so close now that he could see the quickening pulse in the fine skin of her neck above her coral necklace, and her rising chest beneath the fine cotton of her camisole. She swallowed, and he allowed his gaze to linger on the movement in her throat. Such an elegant neck, which was too delicate to hide both her arousal and her fears. Interesting. He raised his eyes to hers again. Her lips parted and her eyes looked alarmed and excited in equal parts.

"Would you like more coffee?"

She looked down at her coffee as if she'd forgotten all about it. She took a sip. He smiled as she tried to regain her focus. "No, thank you." She took another long drink until the cup was drained. He was impressed by her ability to withhold the shudder from its bitterness. She placed the cup onto the table and looked at him with a bright, if reserved, smile. "Well, it's been lovely meeting you."

She was preparing to leave already. He didn't want that. He might not get another chance.

"You seem reluctant to answer my question."

She shook her head. "Question?"

He allowed a grin to briefly touch his lips. He had her. "I wondered what it was that made you so understanding of being a fish out of water, a foreigner."

"Ah, that. Nothing really." She glanced out the window and long seconds passed without her replying. He wondered if her mind had wandered. But when she returned that soft gaze to him, he could see that it was the opposite. She'd been considering the question. He liked that. She gave things due consideration. She wasn't in a rush to return an easy answer. "I guess it's less to do with a place, more to do with a feeling." He couldn't argue with that. She sighed and rose. "I must go now."

He rose too, easily standing a head over her. She looked so fragile, so delicate. He had an impulse to take her into his arms and hold her there, carefully, so as not to crush her. All it would take would be a slight incline of his head to brush his lips against hers. He could see she was thinking the same thing. He stepped away with a smile.

"Of course."

He followed her to the door and stood, watching, as she walked down the stairs. She looked up to the wooded estate beyond, the jut of her jaw strong, her ponytail flicking from side to side as she trotted down the last few rickety wooden steps.

"I forgot," she said, twisting around at the bottom of the stairs.

"What?"

"You wanted to talk to me about the Arab horses, their stables."

He allowed himself a slow, sexy smile. "Next time. When I make you coffee with spices."

She turned away, but not quickly enough to hide the blush which spread across her cheeks. She waved a brief farewell, obviously not trusting herself to speak, and hurried away.

LAUREN COULDN'T GET AWAY FAST ENOUGH. She felt as if she were running from a flame that flickered and darted at will, nearly catching her with every teasing brush against her skin. She didn't stop walking until she entered the cool grandeur of the manor's hall. Only then did she lean back against the closed door and place her hand against her heated cheek. What on earth had just happened? She'd been curious since the first moment she'd seen him. But nothing had prepared her for being within his orbit, seeing him up close. If she'd been a machine, she'd have said he'd flicked on all her switches. Her breathing was coming fast, her heart beat rapidly, but it was more than that. Her entire skin shimmered with a sensual awareness which his presence had created.

"Miss le Harivel? Is anything the matter? Are you all right?" asked the estate manager with a frown, as he passed through to the offices.

She moved forward, away from the door toward the stairs which would take her back to the safety of her suite of rooms. "Of course. Why wouldn't I be?" As she ran up the stairs, she felt more alive from being with Rayan than at any other time she could recall.

Was she all right? She was so far beyond 'all right' that there were no words she knew to describe how she felt. But maybe after another visit to the exotic Rayan, she'd find the words she needed.

She stopped at the top of the stairs, her heart still pounding, but alongside that crept a sense of fear which soon consumed her excitement. There was no getting away from it—the thought of seeing Rayan again scared her. No, she couldn't allow herself another visit. It wouldn't be seemly, it wouldn't be proper. Besides, her father would arrive next week and she knew, for sure, that he *certainly* wouldn't approve.

# CHAPTER 2

Lauren passed the papers over to the estate manager, Jeremy, with a sigh. It was her birthday, and it appeared, it would be business as usual. There would be no celebrations, no one had remembered, least of all her father who was, yet again, a no-show despite his promises. The disappointment bit deep, piercing her usual reserve.

She felt angry with her father and pleased that she'd delegated some of the load she'd carried for him for years to Jeremy. At first she'd felt guilty, but with each passing month she'd felt increasingly resentful at all her father expected of her. And, more than anything, she felt an intense desire to break out, to do something just for herself.

"I think that's the lot, thank you, Jeremy."

She jumped up from her desk and tried to stop herself from looking out the window at the stable yard, scanning it for the man who dominated her mind, day and night. She usually tried to wait until she was alone. But today the sense of unease and frustration which had been festering for months had come to a head, and she was impatient for a glimpse of Rayan. Surely she could treat herself on her birthday to such an innocent indulgence? But, even as her mind framed the word 'innocent', she knew she was fooling herself. There was nothing innocent about her thoughts and reactions to this man. *That* was the reason she'd avoided him.

She looked out the window anyway, scanning first the stable yard then the rest of the estate with the desperation of a woman searching for water in a desert. Nothing. No sign of the man who, it seemed, had also been avoiding her. Because she hadn't seen him since their coffee together. If she hadn't searched the personnel databases, she might have thought he'd left. But she had, and he hadn't.

She glanced at Jeremy, who cast her a look, full of meaning. She turned away from the window and tilted her head to one side, irritated by the disapproving glance.

"What is it, Jeremy?" She folded her arms defensively. She wouldn't let any of the staff get to her. She refused to. "Have you forgotten something?"

Jeremy tapped the sheaf of papers on the desk and slid them into his leather briefcase. When he looked up, his expression had assumed its usual deferential smile. But she wasn't fooled.

"No, Miss le Harivel. Everything is accounted for. I'll have these papers taken to the solicitors straight away, and the money wired to your father… as usual." The length of time before adding 'as usual' revealed his disapproval. For once, Lauren had to agree with him. Her father siphoned off more money from the estate than she, or her accountant, was comfortable with, but she'd always agreed to his demands, despite the fact she now held the casting vote. She didn't see she had any choice but to smooth the rough path her father made through life.

"Thank you, Jeremy."

He rose, his tall, slender figure rising above her. "Is there anything else I can do?"

She hesitated, but she had to know. "Yes, I haven't seen the new stable-hand for a while. My father wanted us to nurture our Arab horses and, I have to say, he was doing good work. Could you tell me where he's gone?"

Jeremy's smile froze, and he assumed a frosty expression. "He's been moved, Miss le Harivel."

"Moved? Why? He was hired as a stable-hand, wasn't he? And given the room above the stable. So why has he been moved?"

Jeremy licked his lips while his eyes flickered, revealing his disquiet. "It was considered... *preferable*."

She hated the way he hesitated before picking a word, which was obviously his second choice.

"Preferable to what?"

"To hanging around the estate, so close to the house, so close to *you*. We thought he might be making a nuisance of himself."

"Did you now?" If it wasn't her father, it was the estate staff, determined to run her life. Well, it had to stop now. Any thought of trying to hide her interest had obviously been ineffectual, and she didn't see there was any point in prolonging it. "Well, I'd like him back, working at the stable. When my father returns, he'll want to see his horses in peak condition. See to it, please."

Jeremy dipped his head in reluctant agreement. "As you wish."

"I *do* wish!"

Lauren watched him disappear, trying to rein in the unusual anger which darted through her body, igniting it into action. But she never acted, did she? Her role was to be calm, work hard, and do her duty, and she'd always done what was expected of her. But then, what was the alternative? Throw herself at a man who wouldn't look twice at someone like her? No, her father was right. Men were only ever interested in her for who she was, rather than for herself. It was always her money and status that men found alluring, never her. Why would it be any different now?

She returned to her desk and sat down, feeling the hope and excitement evaporate, replaced by disappointment and rejection. She took a deep breath and stared at the blank computer screen for a few moments before jiggling the mouse into action. As the screen flickered into life, Lauren couldn't help wishing her own world would come to life with the same ease.

IT WAS hot in the small room above the stables. Rayan lay on the bed, tidily made with old fashioned sheets and blankets—it seemed a duvet was too modern for this estate—with his arms hooked under his head, and stared up at the ceiling. All the windows were open to the heat of the summer night, which was trapped in that small space. He made no attempt to lighten the twilight. Instead, he lay listening to the sounds of the English birds, so soothing and gentle, and thought about Lauren.

Although the staff had obviously decided to put as much space between him and Lauren as possible, he had watched her from a distance. She was not at all as he'd imagined her to be, nothing like his pre-conceived notions of what a spoiled only child of an English aristocrat would be like.

In the only photos he'd found of her online, she'd always been in the background, slightly out of focus beside her father, who commanded the photographer's attention with his wide smiles, and raised champagne glass. Written and verbal accounts had also been curiously vague. He'd imagined an aloof woman with a superior air. Nothing could have been further from the truth.

He could understand why people's descriptions had been

vague, because there was nothing showy about her, and she had been easily overlooked when in the company of her father and friends. And they were the only times she'd been in the public eye. But, away from her father, he had to admit she shone. Not with the strident beam of a spotlight maybe, but with a subtler, more gentle, diffuse light. It was the kind of light which, only when it was withdrawn, did you realize quite how bright it was.

He grunted, and rubbed his eyes. It was a ridiculous notion. But, try as he might, he couldn't help thinking of how that steady light, which shone from behind her eyes, quickened at times, revealing a strength and latent passion which made him think seducing her wouldn't be so hard. The passion he'd caught glimpses of was entirely untapped. All he had to do was figure out how to coax it out.

His mind wandered into a daydream which featured her calling his name in that deep and sexy voice of hers. He groaned but allowed his daydream to continue until he heard a sound outside his window. He sat up suddenly and turned to the window.

The stable apartment guarded the stables and was built so that the occupant could hear everyone and every horse coming and going through the stable yard. And now he heard a sound which he shouldn't have. The stables were out of bounds for everyone at night, apart from himself. And he could hear soft footfalls walking on the cobbled yard below, hesitating, and then moving on. It sounded as if the person was heading towards the lake. By the time he reached the window, whoever it was had been swallowed up by the inky twilight.

Rayan pulled on a shirt, quietly opened his door, and descended the worn wooden steps. He turned his back to the manor house and walked stealthily toward the trees, which separated the stables from the lake. Despite his fast pace, he didn't see anyone in the twists and turns of the path. Long grasses edged the pathway and the trees, which loomed darkly overhead, cut out any lingering light from the sky. But his other senses were heightened, just as they would be on a desert hunt, and he was aware of the disturbed calls of birds and their movement as they rose in alarm from the trees. Somebody was entering private land, and he was determined to find out who it was.

Suddenly the trees thinned, and he stopped abruptly, lingering under their shadows as he looked out to the silhouette of a figure standing stock still, gazing across the lake. It wasn't the silhouette of a man, and it wasn't the silhouette of an intruder—it was the unmistakable figure of the woman whose image refused to leave his mind.

For a moment he wondered whether he should approach, but caution made him stay put. But it wasn't only caution. He wanted to see what she would do, unobserved.

The answer was nothing. Long minutes passed in which she stood, her slight figure upright as usual, her hands hanging loosely by her side, as she looked out across the forbidding depths of the lake to a dark, uneven smudge of trees on the farther shore. Above the uneven line of trees rose distant hills, topped by an inky, star-sprinkled sky.

He followed her gaze but saw nothing unusual in the view. By day it was a beautiful scene—the deep blue of the lake reflecting the ancient trees, which ensured its privacy from the rest of the estate's park. But now, there was nothing but shadows, layers of dark upon dark and a sky which held nothing but mystery. Suddenly he understood. It wasn't the view she admired, but the privacy of the place which had drawn her. She was here to think, or reflect upon something, drawn to the lake by its mysterious quietness and seclusion.

Instinctively, he respected that need for quiet solace. Yes, he needed to seduce her, but not here, not now. He stepped away and turned, catching his shirt on a dry piece of overhanging twig. It snapped and the sound rang out into the night.

She turned round, and he knew from the twists and turns of her head that she hadn't seen him in the shadows. He could leave now, and she'd be none the wiser that he'd witnessed her need for silence and space.

"Who's there?" He was surprised not to hear any fear in her voice, only that low, sexy sureness, which belied her appearance.

Impulsively, he stepped forward. "It's me, Rayan."

"Oh! What are you doing here?" She turned to face him fully, but still he could barely discern her features. "Are you following me?"

"Yes. I believe it's part of my job description to check out intruders."

She gave a low laugh—either of amusement or relief, he couldn't tell—and then twisted back to look at the view. She heaved a sigh and then glanced around at him once more.

"Of course, you're just doing a job. Making sure no one is trespassing near our horses. Although I had the feeling that your job description has altered since we last met. "

The change from authoritative mistress of the manor to a more familiar tone encouraged him to step out from the shadows and walk over to her. It seemed he hadn't jeopardized his mission; in fact, this might be the perfect opportunity to further it. He stood a little apart from her and followed her gaze out across the lake.

"After our last meeting, I was given other jobs to keep me away from the stables—away from you. I don't think they liked it."

"*They*? Who are *they*?"

He turned to her with a smile. "*They* are the people who run this estate."

"*I* run this estate."

He decided silence was the best reply. Maybe he'd said too much, but she had to know that, while she might run the estate, *she* was being run by other people. No doubt people who were tasked with keeping an eye on her by her father. Her father might prefer to leave a trail of broken women and promises across the world's luxury playgrounds, but he still wanted to control her.

He looked in the opposite direction, determined to remain silent, determined to show her the truth about her position in the family estate. Suddenly, he felt her hand on his arm. He snapped his head back to see her eyes, gray in the twilight, looking up at him with such a mixture of vulnerability and pride that it somehow circumnavigated his defenses and moved him deep inside.

"*I* run this estate," she said. "It's *me*. Not my father, not anyone else."

He was acutely aware of her hand, which still lingered on his arm. It sent skitters of sensation through his body, igniting impulses which he'd thought long dead. He swallowed, forcing himself to focus on anything other than the touch of her arm, and hoping by not moving that she'd keep it there.

"Then perhaps you should tell them," he said eventually.

He noticed she didn't lift her hand from his arm. "They should know already."

"It seems they don't."

"What makes you say that?"

"The way they do as they like without consulting you."

"You think I didn't instruct them to reassign your duties?"

He held his gaze steady. "I know you didn't."

"Hm," she grunted, sending a flame of desire into his gut and lower. He couldn't help imagining her making that same sound, close into his ear, hard against his chest, as he pleasured her. At last she withdrew her arm and, plunging her hands into her pockets, turned back to the view. "You're right. I didn't." Her tone had stiffened. He regretted revealing the truth to her now. He wanted to feel her touch again, the warmth in her voice, her soft glance on him once more.

"They were trying to look after you." He smiled encouragingly, trying to dispel the solemn mood which had fallen over her. "Keep you away from dangerous foreigners like me." He grinned. She looked up at him, but she wasn't smiling.

"I'm a grown woman—I don't need looking after. And maybe it's something foreign I want. Besides, foreign isn't always dangerous. And, anyway, I think I can make up my own mind."

He sucked in a harsh breath. He could make a move now; her words were like an open invitation. But it seemed a greater need over-rode his mission. He also wanted to look after her.

"I'm sure you can. But..." He hesitated as he battled inside of himself whether to take advantage of her changed mood, or hold back. It seemed his mind was overridden by something much deeper and stronger, something like the honor with which he'd been inculcated as a child by his mother. "Take care, Lauren," he said softly. "A leap into the unknown is a risky strategy."

There, he'd said it. He'd warned her. Now it was up to her.

She held his gaze for a few moments and then looked back at the lake. The silence was broken only by the soft hoot of an owl and the clatter of some reeds, as a sudden breeze rippled across the water towards them. Suddenly she smiled.

"I used to imagine things like that—sudden gusts of wind which ruffled the water, lifted my hair and caressed my face, or shimmering lights—were ways in which my mother reached out to me."

"Your mother?"

"She died when I was twelve. I used to come here with her. We would picnic during the day. At night we would sit under blankets and watch the swifts fly around, followed by the bats. It was so peaceful after…"

"After?" He prompted.

She sighed. "After life at the manor. My father isn't exactly an easy man to live with."

At the mention of her father, he felt his blood simmer. And he remembered why he was there. "Then I imagine it's easier while he's away."

"In a way. But I had thought he would be here today."

"Why? What's special about today?"

"It's my birthday. Dad said he would be here for my birthday—be here for me," she added.

The anger was swept away by an overwhelming sense of sadness. Suddenly, it all made sense. This quiet spot, this woman so alone amid such a wealthy community, which revolved around her. She was lonely. It tore at the heart of him, and he didn't want that. In fact, he had no idea how the feeling had emerged. It seemed she could get around his defenses. He re-focused, banished the sadness, and sealed off his heart once more. He had a job to do.

"Happy birthday," he said softly. She continued to look ahead at the view.

And then she turned to him. "Thank you. I'm twenty-two. My twenty-first was to have been my big celebratory birthday, but my father missed that as well. He'd promised to make up for it and to be here for this one. But he isn't."

"I'm glad."

She shot her head around and faced him. "Why?"

"Because then I wouldn't have the opportunity to be here, alone with you, on such a beautiful night."

She smiled and her face lit up the darkness. "That's kind of you to say so."

"I mean it."

"What are you doing here, Rayan? What are you doing on the le Harivel estate, buried in the Norfolk countryside?"

Her question took him by surprise. "Working, of course."

"But you don't seem like someone who works with horses. You don't have the air of someone who is accustomed to being told what to do."

He couldn't help but smile. "You're right. I love horses, and know them well, but at home my life is different."

"In what way?"

How had the conversation turned so that it was her interrogating him? "I run businesses." It was a form of the truth. "I wanted time out."

"And have you got what you wanted from your time out?"

*Nearly, not quite.* He didn't know when he'd get to see her again, given the determination of her staff to keep her away from him. He had to force the issue.

"Mostly. But it's time for me to move on. I don't get the impression I'm welcome here, and I need to return to my country."

"You are welcome to remain here. I'm in control of the estate and if I say you are welcome, you are!"

"Thank you. But I've made arrangements already to return to Ahmar."

"Oh, right! I remember you mentioning Ahmar before and I couldn't think why I'd heard of it."

He frowned. "Nor I. It's a small country."

"Small maybe, but my father had… interests in it. He's been there. The way he described it sounded very exotic. I'd love to see it."

Rayan was surprised. Why hadn't Madaniya told any of her brothers that she'd brought her lover to their country? But of course, she'd have known they wouldn't have approved. "You should visit some time."

She smiled. "Maybe I will. He described how rich in history your country is. He brought back some beautiful artifacts."

Rayan's humor descended another notch. How dare the man take away things belonging to his own country? "Is that right?" he asked slowly.

"Yes. Maybe… Maybe you'd like to see them sometime."

"I would. But I'll be leaving on Wednesday—two days' time." He hadn't made arrangements, but first thing in the morning he would.

"Oh! So you're here for only one more night?" He nodded, and she turned away. He was gratified to see disappointment writ large across her face.

"Yes. One more night. Anyway, I want to know about *you*," he pressed. "And what's holding you here when you don't appear to be happy."

She bristled a little and moved away. He wondered if he'd gone too far, but then she sighed. "You're right. I guess I'm not happy. And I guess I haven't been happy for a long time so it feels normal. When I used to come here with my mother, we'd look out to the hills beyond the trees and we'd talk about the world which lay beyond them. And that's what I still do—imagine what lies beyond."

"But you must know now, you're an adult. You must have been there."

"I've been there, but hardly anywhere else. To me it remains a symbol of all that I don't have, all that I don't know, all that I need." She faced him once more "Sometimes… Sometimes it seems to me that I haven't yet found my home."

"Then why don't you leave? Why don't you leave this place, find out what's beyond the boundaries, find out where you're meant to be?" He hadn't meant to ask that, but he was so moved by this woman who, despite appearing to have everything, it seemed had nothing.

She was silent for a few moments. "My father needs me." The words were clipped, as if she was equally unconvinced. At that moment a lop-sided waning moon rose above the trees, casting its long-promised light over the lake, and revealing her features, her lips slightly apart. He was filled with an overwhelming desire to kiss her. He moved closer to her, and she didn't step away. He was so close now that he could see the moonlight reflected in her eyes, glancing off her pale skin, turning her hair to silver.

He reached out and gently touched her cheek with his finger. It felt like silk. He hardly knew whether he was about to bring her face closer to his or move away. And, it seemed, she didn't know which way it would go, either. He could make his move now, but there was something so defenseless about her eyes which stopped him. He withdrew his hand and shifted away.

"I should leave now." He glanced at her before looking back at the lake again firmly. "I'll leave you to your peace and quiet."

She didn't reply, so he stepped away and walked up the small grassy bank back to the path.

"Rayan! You said I should be careful about yearning for something foreign, for something unknown. I want you to know that I'm beyond being careful now. Because I've had enough peace and quiet to last me a lifetime."

He stopped walking, and closed his eyes as he winced at the invitation. There was no doubt that that was what it was. He turned to her slowly.

"Lauren..." he said, her name slipping from his lips like a

caress. He shook his head. Something had shifted between them. He'd wanted to increase their intimacy, but it hadn't gone according to plan. Because it wasn't physical intimacy he'd got, but emotional, and he wanted none of that. After he'd done what he'd set out to do, he'd cut her out of his life. That was the plan. There would be no returning to the vulnerable woman at the lakeside, who held the memory of her mother close and her dreams closer. He winced. He couldn't do it. Not now, anyway.

"Goodnight."

Without waiting for her to answer, he continued along the path, up the steps to his room above the stable, and closed the door firmly. But he couldn't stop himself from standing by the window, in the shadows, and watching her walk under his window a little while later. She might have got under his skin, but he'd also got under hers, and the next time they met he'd be sure not to make the same mistake twice.

By setting his date of departure he'd condensed the time frame, and set a ticking clock going which would bring them together. He'd make sure they meet the next night and then, when they were alone together, this time he wouldn't walk away.

# CHAPTER 3

All the following day, Lauren had thought of nothing else but her encounter with Rayan. As she'd been listening to Jeremy drone on about the accounts, she'd remembered Rayan's expression when the moon had risen. It had been obscured before, only partly guessed at by his words. But there was no mistaking the look in his eye when the moonlight flooded the lake—he wanted her in the same way she wanted him.

As she'd inspected some new estate housing, making sure the builders had kept to the architect's brief, she'd re-lived the feeling she'd experienced at the sight of his lips parting in a soft smile at something she'd said.

And, as she'd returned to an empty manor house, she contemplated his departure. He'd said he was leaving on Wednesday. That left only one night to be with him. Tonight. So she'd slipped a note under his door. Now the only question is, would he come?

. . .

AT THE APPOINTED HOUR, Lauren stood in the hall at the foot of the stairs. She'd dismissed her staff, so she was completely alone in the house. The grandfather clock in the hallway ticked away the minutes until the ornate brass hour hand clicked onto eight and the clock chimed the hour. Lauren wiped her hands nervously down her silk dress. She rarely wore dresses, but tonight she wanted something from this exotic man who'd come into her life unexpectedly and planned to leave just as suddenly. And she was determined to make sure he didn't leave before she got it. She hoped the silk dress—and the way it draped becomingly around her petite frame—would make up for her own lack of allure.

The minutes ticked on past the hour, but still no one came to her door. And then, suddenly, she heard a movement behind her. She twisted around and saw Rayan closing the door which led to the service wing and the rear entrance.

"Lauren," he said, in that deep exotic voice which ruffled her skin. "You're waiting for me."

She felt off guard. She'd expected him to arrive by the front door and had not intended to be caught waiting for him. But, of course, he was an employee, and had entered from the service wing of the manor.

"Rayan!" She cleared her throat, noting her voice sounded hoarse and uncertain. There seemed little point in denying it. "Yes, I am. I thought…" She hesitated as she tried to pull together her scattered senses. "I thought I wouldn't hear you upstairs in my library. And…" She trailed off again, realizing that she was about to admit that she'd dismissed all her household staff for the night.

He came and stood close to her, scrutinized her face, and then glanced behind him. "And there's no one around to show me in. The service wing is empty. Usually there's at least a skeleton staff at night."

She swallowed. It seemed there was to be no fooling him. "I gave them leave. I wanted to be alone."

"And yet you're not alone. You invited me here." He cocked his head to one side. "You wanted to be alone with me?"

Her words wouldn't emerge. It was as if they were strangled by emotion. All she could do was nod her head.

He gave a quick smile. "Good. Because I had exactly the same thought."

"I… I've had some supper laid out for us upstairs, in my sitting room." She paused. "After our talk last night I thought you'd be interested in seeing some things I have there."

His lips tweaked into a smile. "I'm sure I would." Before she could wonder exactly what he meant, he took command of the situation—something a mere stable-hand would never do—and waved his hand, indicating the stairs. "After you."

Her best high heels clicked on the parquet floor before dulling on the thickly carpeted stair runner as she ascended the sweep of stairs to the wide landing, lined with portraits of her ancestors, and opened the paneled door to her private sitting room.

As she walked across the room to where a group of overstuffed china blue sofas surrounded a coffee table, she could have sworn she felt his gaze on her back. When she turned around, he'd closed the door behind him and was looking at her through narrowed eyes. A wave of heat rose and flooded her normally pale cheeks with a telltale response.

"Nice." He wasn't looking at the room.

"Thank you." She gripped the back of a sofa for support, determined to interpret his words in the least personal way possible. "I spend most of my time here."

He raised an eyebrow. "You have a large house and yet you choose to spend your time in one room?"

She shrugged. She refused to be completely open with

him. "I have a lot of work to do and so I choose to do it here. It's quieter. And..." she trailed off as she considered why she was here. "It's mine."

"I understand." He glanced around. "It looks more personal, more intimate." The way he said the word 'intimate' sent shivers down her spine. "You don't feel isolated?"

She couldn't give him a direct answer, not without lying, and she never did that. "I have regular meetings with my estate manager here. And I can see who comes and goes if I wish."

She regretted her last words instantly. He glanced to the window and walked over to it, pushing back part of the swathe of heavy curtain. "You have a good view of the stables." He turned to her with a small smile.

"Yes," she said, in a rush of hastily caught breath. She fisted her hands. She had to get a grip. She was acting like a teenager. She gave a quick smile and pointed to the chairs. "Please, take a seat." She kept her eyes lowered. "Would you care for anything to eat?"

She made the mistake of looking up, catching his eye, and could not look away from that intense look. He walked slowly over to her, around the chairs. Her heart was thumping with every step he took towards her. Then he leaned over the table, lifted her hand from the silver cloche, and placed it between both of his large, calloused hands.

"I'm not here to waste time, Lauren."

She sucked in a ragged breath, desperately trying to calm her quickened heartbeat.

"Then what are you here for?"

His gaze heated and remained fixed on her. "You."

"Oh." She exhaled with a slight grunt.

"That's why you invited me, wasn't it?"

She nodded. He tugged her closer and she bumped lightly against him, but she didn't move away. With his other hand, he lightly caressed her cheek, his eyes roaming over her face as if he admired what he saw.

"Tell me now, Lauren, if I've imagined this... feeling between us—tell me if I've misunderstood?"

She shook her head. There was no way she could deny it. Every part of her—inside and out—was making it very clear to her, and no doubt to him, that he had this *very* right.

He lowered his face to hers and she could feel the warmth of his breath against her cheek, could smell his aftershave and other scents—leather, ambergris and something utterly indefinable which made her mouth water. Then he did what she'd imagined him doing since the morning she'd first seen him. He pressed his lips to hers.

She felt his sharp intake of breath against her lips before they moved over hers, caressing her, stirring every part of her into life. Shivers of desire coursed through her body, finding places inside her she'd firmly repressed for years, sparking them into life. She moved her lips over his with increasing urgency as she inhaled his masculine scent and responded to the rough feel of his hands against her cheeks.

Then she felt the tip of his tongue against hers. The kiss deepened and all thought flew out the window. Their tongues tangled and their breathing became more ragged as his hands lowered from her face and slipped around her, caressing the small of her back. Instinctively, she shifted closer to him, her hips brushing his before she settled against him, hardly realizing what she was doing until she felt his erection pressed against her stomach. A flood of heat and wet washed through her before settling into an insistent throbbing in her sex.

She cried out as he lifted his mouth from her lips, thinking he was going to move away. But, it appeared, that was the last thing on his mind. She threw her head back, and he took full advantage of it to taste her skin and to kiss her throat before descending lower still. He trailed his tongue down her chest to her breasts. She hadn't even been aware that he'd undone the buttons of her dress until she looked down to see his mouth on her small breast, covered only in a plain white cotton bra. She wasn't prepared for the raft of sensations which flooded her body. If she'd fooled herself as to her intentions earlier in the evening, there was no way she could now. She wanted him. Pure and simple.

She gasped as the wet heat of his mouth covered her breast and the gasp turned into a moan as he hooked his finger under her bra, pulled it down, and suckled hard on her nipple. She cried out at the unexpected sensation. "Rayan!"

He lifted his head and looked up at her, cocking his head to one side.

"Do you want to stop? I thought—"

She didn't want to hear what he thought, so she shook her head vehemently and pulled his head back to her breast, all thought of propriety gone.

"No," she murmured between gasps, as he continued to suckle and play with first one breast and then the other. "I don't want you to stop. It's the last thing I want you to do."

And when he lifted his head again, it wasn't to stop, but to press his mouth to hers in a passionate kiss which eclipsed the first one, because she knew now what magic his lips could create on her body. She staggered back under the pressure of his mouth on hers until she found herself hard against the desk with nowhere else to go.

His hands roamed freely around her body, just as hers did his. It seemed that they both felt the same urgency. As the kiss continued, growing in intensity, she undid his shirt and slipped her hands underneath, relishing the feel of his taut back muscles under her fingertips. Her touch ignited something more in him and, when she looked down, she found her dress was entirely unbuttoned. He pulled her dress aside and stepped away as if to admire her.

Naked except for her plain underwear, she suddenly felt unsure as she swayed, feeling lost without his support. His hands were around her again before she could stumble, and he lifted her onto the desk. She tried, without success, to shift away some of the desk's clutter on which she sat.

"Allow me," he murmured against her lips. He lifted her into his arms and, with one swift movement, swept everything off the desk and onto the floor.

He placed her back onto the desk once more and caressed her naked thighs, before sweeping his fingers over her knickers, between her legs, where the dampness revealed exactly how much she wanted him. Shyly, she opened her legs to allow his fingers better access.

He grunted, kissed her deeply, and then pulled away. Her eyes fell to his erection, which was straining at his jeans.

He muttered words in a foreign language she didn't understand, but they sounded like a curse. She pushed his hair from his eyes and his gaze held a savagery which took her breath away. He looked as if he wanted to devour her, to annihilate her and she wanted whatever he would give her—anything to be transported away into a life of passion far from her own lonely and dull existence.

"Are you sure you want this, Lauren?" he asked in a husky voice that exuded sex.

"Yes, Christ, yes. It's all I want!" She rolled her forehead against his, needing to feel the pressure of his skin against hers. "I want you to make love to me. I want you inside me, I want you to show me how a woman should feel."

He needed no further encouragement or permission, and within seconds he'd freed her of her underwear, and her knickers were tossed to one side, her bra to the other. Then he took over from her unpractised fumblings and undid his jeans. He pushed them down, together with his briefs, revealing that part of him she'd spent sleepless nights imagining. It was thicker and longer than she'd imagined. Briefly she wondered how on earth it would fit inside her. But she didn't have to wonder long.

He guided her legs, and she wrapped them around him as he positioned himself against her. He pulled her to him and with one deep push, entered her. She cried out, and he stopped suddenly, only part way inside her.

"Lauren?" He pulled back and looked at her. "What—"

She stopped his question with a kiss. She wanted no discussion about her virginity. She simply wanted it gone, like a symbol of her old life, which was no life. She wriggled, and pulled him further toward her, willing him to push past the barrier which symbolized everything she wanted broken down.

Whether she'd reassured him, or whether he couldn't stop himself, he thrust carefully into her with a slow, decisive movement, which was exactly what she wanted. She hadn't expected the sudden blast of numbing pain and couldn't help crying out again. He stopped moving while he kissed her again, and she slowly relaxed as her body accommodated herself to him. When he lifted his head, he pushed a lock of hair away from her face and frowned.

"It's okay, it's what I want," she said, answering the unanswered question.

His expression was tense; she could see he could barely restrain himself, and for a moment she didn't know whether he'd continue or withdraw. He withdrew. Suddenly scared he'd withdraw all the way, she pressed her mouth to his chest, his neck, and kissed him, wriggling further onto him, wincing a little as she did so. He kept apart and placed his hand between them and then lowered it until he found the place he wanted and gently massaged it. Any pain was soon obliterated by waves of pure pleasure. Sensing her relaxation, he kissed her before thrusting deeply inside her. This time there was no obstruction and she gasped as the tempo of the thrusting increased, sending her to the brink of an unimagined place where she knew she wanted to be.

Suddenly there was an explosion of light and a burst of sensation shot through her. She fell against him. He held her tightly as he continued to thrust, until his breath caught and he gave short thrusting motions, and she knew he'd come deep inside of her.

There could be no doubt as he withdrew and the discomfort of her first sexual experience overpowered the pleasure, settling into a throbbing soreness as his seed trickled from her.

He kissed her and muttered words she didn't understand under his breath.

"Tell me what it is you're saying, Rayan. Did I disappoint you?"

"No, no." He kissed her. "Of course not. You are beautiful. But I had not expected..." He trailed off. "I did not imagine..."

"That I was a virgin?"

He closed his eyes briefly and nodded. "If I'd known, I..." He paused and shook his head, as if confused. "I'm sorry."

"There's nothing to be sorry for. I wanted you to make love to me. It was the most amazing experience of my life." And, truthfully, it was. Any discomfort had been more than compensated for by the pleasure she'd gained. And not just sexual pleasure, but being able to let down her guard and be herself with this hypnotic man. The only thing she regretted was that the sex had been unprotected. In the heat of the moment she'd forgotten all about the condoms she'd bought only that morning and placed in her beside drawer. They hadn't even made it to the bedroom.

He shot her a quick smile, which was extinguished all too soon. She felt her own happiness dim at his obvious unease. Was it only her virginity which made him regret making love to her, or was it something else?

He helped her off the desk and she pulled her dress around herself awkwardly and folded her arms.

"This shouldn't have happened," he said, pushing his fingers through his unruly hair and turning away from her. "I am leaving tomorrow. It shouldn't have happened."

She reached out to touch his shoulder, but didn't make contact. Her hand hovered close to him briefly before she let it drop to her side. Despite the physical intimacy of sex, the emotional intimacy didn't seem appropriate.

"I knew that, and I wanted you anyway. It was as simple as that."

He twisted his head to look at her, frowning. "And you truly have no regrets?"

She only had one regret, and that she would not tell him. She shook her head. "Only one."

"What's that?"

"That you have your back to me, and you're not kissing me." Maybe she had two regrets, but she decided to keep the other one from him.

He shook his head and turned to her, and she could tell from his smile that something had changed. Whatever had filled his mind before—doubts, regrets, whatever—had now gone.

He swept his fingers along her cheek, and she liked the way he looked at her. "You are so beautiful."

She frowned. "No, I'm not."

He stepped away from her and plucked his shirt from the floor where he'd tossed it. "You are. You just don't know it because you've been shut up here, like a fairytale princess in a castle, abandoned."

The image shocked her momentarily before she realized he was right.

"Only visited," he continued, "from time to time, by a father who doesn't see your beauty, doesn't value your worth."

Part of her couldn't believe him, but it was the smallest part, because she knew that her life had changed forever that evening. Her whole life she'd yearned for an intimacy and a connection... for love. She didn't know if she'd found love with Rayan, but she knew that she'd found something that made her feel cherished and valued like she'd never felt before. It was all she'd ever wanted.

And in that moment, she knew she would do anything to be with him. She watched him collect his things before he turned to look at her, his expression intense. In two strides, he bridged the gap between them and gave her a passionate kiss. He stepped away.

"I want you to come with me. Think of it as a holiday, if you wish, but come with me. I'll leave now before your staff return, but please, think about it." He kissed her long and hard. "We can make love all day, and all night long, without fear of anyone walking in."

Without waiting for her to reply, he left the room. Lauren listened to his retreating steps and knew that there had been no need to reply. Her heart was made up. She'd persuade her mind tomorrow.

THE FOLLOWING DAY FLEW BY. There were arrangements to make, things to put into place, all without telling anyone she was leaving. They'd find out soon enough, but she didn't want to risk anyone, including her father, talking her around. She knew she was letting her heart rule her head, but loved how that felt. Besides, Rayan had been correct. Her staff knew how to run the family business and her father, as head of the company, would simply have to assume the roles he'd been shirking for years. Besides, she might be back in a few weeks after her 'holiday'—for that was how she'd framed it in her emails. Whether it was to be a holiday, or something more permanent, she didn't have a clue and was all the more excited because of it.

Finally, everything had been done. Her bag was packed, and she'd left a letter for her father on the desk in her father's first-floor library where her staff would see it. It was the only message in which she'd given her destination. With everything done, she was impatient to see Rayan. She hurried outside, before the walk turned into a run as she passed along the shadowy paths of the circuitous route that she knew he would follow to the stables. She was surprised that there was no outside light at the top of the apartment steps. She looked around, but there was nobody there. She walked up the steps and knocked, but there was no answer. She tried the handle and to her surprise it opened and she entered his apartment, but it was empty—his things were gone.

She clutched her throat as panic threatened to overwhelm her. He wouldn't have gone without her. He wouldn't. Maybe she'd missed him. That was it. He'd gone to see her at the manor by a different route.

She ran back down the steps and hurriedly returned to the manor. She knew where he'd go—to the room in which they'd made love the previous night. She burst into it, looked around and her heart sank. It was empty. She continued through the adjoining door to her bedroom. Again, nothing. Suddenly she heard the door to the downstairs library close and heard footsteps ascending the stairs. She waited in the bedroom and Rayan suddenly appeared and, without hesitation, entered her bedroom and closed the door.

"I've just been looking for you. I thought—"

Before she could finish her sentence, he had his arms around her waist and was kissing her so thoroughly that she forgot what she was thinking. All she was aware of was how right this felt, and how much she needed this connection with him. Eventually he pulled away, caressing her bottom as he brought her hard against him, revealing how much he wanted her, too.

"You didn't think I would leave you behind, did you?" he said in a gravelly voice.

"I didn't know."

"Are your bags packed?"

She swallowed nervously, but nodded. "Yes, but—"

He placed his finger against her lips. "No buts."

"My father relies on me. He'll be devastated."

His face froze into a mask of distaste she couldn't understand. "Your father, who didn't even bother to return to you for your birthday?"

She opened her mouth to defend her father, but there were no words, no thoughts, nothing she could say to defend the man who had always failed her.

Rayan's grip on her arms tightened. "We must leave now."

"I'm scared, Rayan," she whispered.

"There's nothing to fear. We have a connection, surely that tells you something?"

"It tells me I'm losing my mind."

He shook his head, his shadowy features lightening before passing into shadows with each shake. "You're not losing mind. You are experiencing life. I've shown you what it is like, now it is up to you to take it. Think about those lands over the hills. It's your time now, Lauren, and you must take the opportunity."

Words she could have denied, words she could have ignored, but when he pressed his lips to hers, all thoughts of defense, all thoughts of resistance flew out the window. She weakened into his arms, and he supported her. And the kiss deepened, and she moaned as his hands explored her body, lifting her dress. She felt his erection pressed into her stomach and knew that, at that moment, he could do whatever he liked with her. She was entirely in his thrall. There was no fight in her, no desire to be assertive in their love-making. If he wanted to take her, he could.

He must have sensed her surrender because he quickly disposed of her knickers and slid his hands against her sex and caressed her, sending shivers of excitement sparking through her body. His finger slid along the length of her wet sex, and his tongue mimicked the motions of his finger, circling before plunging inside. She moaned and suddenly he'd lifted her, her legs around him, as he took her over to the bed.

She lay in the moonlight, her white dress rucked up around her waist, her legs open in invitation, as she watched him quickly undress. He didn't say a word. There was no kiss, no words, no gentle caress. He simply lifted her hips firmly and pushed his cock deep inside of her. She gasped at the firm intrusion, the blatant intent, and gasped again, this time from pure pleasure, as he pulled out and pushed back inside of her. His eyes never left hers as he edged her toward orgasm.

She felt as if her body was disintegrating, and she called out his name as he came inside her.

"You're mine now, *habibti*." He kissed her. "Now"—he lay back on the bed, watching her—"get ready. We leave immediately."

## CHAPTER 4

"We're here."

Rayan's voice came to her through a haze. At first she thought she was at home, on her estate, and he was calling to her through the trees. But she couldn't see him. She began to run, but then the trees vanished and she suddenly found herself on the edge of her known world—a precipice before her, darkness behind her and nowhere to go. And then she heard her name called again.

"Lauren, we're here." His tone was more insistent now.

She opened her eyes with a start and struggled to calm her breathing.

"It's okay, Lauren, we'll be landing soon."

Slowly, her surroundings filtered through her panicked consciousness. The loud, low hum of the airplane vibrated through her body, and the comforting reassurance of his hand on her arm made her look up at him and meet his concerned gaze.

"Rayan," she murmured, before turning her gaze to the view outside the window. Rather than being comforted by her reality, she again felt the sense that she was falling into the unknown. Problem was, she couldn't stop herself—it was an unknown that she wanted.

"Are you all right?" he asked.

She nodded, her gaze still fixed on the brilliant azure waters below them and an approaching coastline of white sand and palm trees. Behind it lay an adobe-colored city, covering the central hill and beyond, before it merged into a desert which stretched as far as the eye could see. She looked back at Rayan and gave him a quick, uncertain smile.

"Sure." Shakily, she raked her hair off her face and leaned back against the seat, allowing the air conditioning to cool her heated skin. "Sure," she repeated, this time with more conviction. "I was in a deep sleep."

He released his grip on her hand and followed her gaze out to the city, suddenly exposed as the plane banked for its final approach to the airport. Lauren was struck by the absence of high-rise towers and glass. There were no flashes of light as the sun reflected off glass buildings, no towering office skyscrapers, only an organic flow of adobe-colored rooftops, terraces, walls and chimneys as the ancient buildings tumbled over the landscape.

"It's beautiful, isn't it?" murmured Rayan.

Lauren was struck by his softer tone, and suddenly thought how little she knew about him. But that was what she wanted, wasn't it? An adventure with someone who gave her what she'd craved for years—attention. "Do you live in the city?"

His expression changed instantly. "No."

"Then, where do you live? There doesn't look to be anything much beyond the city, except desert."

"That's where I live."

She sighed. She guessed she'd have to get used to his brief answers.

"And that's where we're heading?"

He nodded.

Nerves fluttered in her stomach. If she didn't like it, she'd leave, she told herself firmly. As far as the estate staff were concerned, she'd taken a few weeks holiday on an impulse. Everyone was entitled to a few weeks' vacation, weren't they? Lauren swallowed hard. She looked back at the window as she tried to absorb the fact that she was going to be spending her vacation with Rayan in the middle of a desert. Somehow Rayan had omitted to tell her this before. The desert? How could *she*, coming from an English manor house where the world was always green and mild, stay in the desert, even if it were only for a few weeks? It was so... so *alien*.

"You said you wanted to see the world," Rayan said, his tone now harder than his earlier, gentle one.

"Yes, I do." She looked out the window as they approached the airport runway, beyond and either side of which was nothing but mile upon mile, upon hundreds of miles, of desert. She swallowed hard. She knew it would take every inch of her stubbornness to cope with whatever lay ahead of her. But it *was* what she wanted, wasn't it? The question remained unanswered in her mind because it wasn't as simple as a 'yes' or a 'no'. The answer lay somewhere in between, and the only way she'd know for sure was by continuing on the journey she'd begun. Trouble was, she now realized it wouldn't be as easy as she'd imagined from the luxury and safety of her English home.

Suddenly she felt the touch of his finger upon her cheek, and she turned to him. Gone was the challenge and hardness in his eyes. Instead was a softness which melted away her fears. His eyes searched hers for a moment before he gently pressed his lips to hers. The kiss held a tenderness which he rarely showed. He seemed to veer between extreme coldness and intense tenderness. She was captivated by him in both states, whether she wanted to be or not. She twisted in her seat and cupped his face with her hands and deepened the kiss. This was what she wanted. This was the freedom she yearned for. And in that moment, she thought she could cope with anything.

"Madam, please, do up your seatbelt. We are about to land."

With her cheeks flushed with embarrassment, Lauren sat back in her seat, and clipped the belt which had released as she'd twisted round to kiss Rayan. She smiled briefly at the flight attendant, who had quickly taken her seat.

Rayan took hold of her hand. It would be okay.

SHE STILL HELD that thought tight in her mind as they collected their bags and walked out of the air-conditioned building into the unrelenting mid-day heat. They trundled their bags to the car rental and joined the end of the line. Lauren was just thinking how strange it was to queue for anything, when an official approached Rayan with a strangely deferential air and spoke quickly to him. Rayan turned to her. "Follow me."

They walked into an air-conditioned office where the stranger pushed aside the paperwork and handed a key to Rayan. He seemed to be apologizing for something, over and over. What, she did not know. Rayan stopped him with a brief, perfunctory command. She opened her eyes wide in surprise. Wouldn't he get into trouble talking that way to these fearsome looking guards armed with guns? But from the anxious looks on the guards' faces, it didn't appear so. Whatever was going on was swiftly over and, within minutes, they were outside in the heat once more, walking past the queue of people and into the car park, where the official opened the car door for Rayan, before bowing to Lauren.

"I trust you enjoy your stay here, madam," the official said in perfect but heavily accented English.

"Thank you, I'm sure I will." Or rather, she *hoped* she would.

Rayan took her bags and placed them into the boot of the car, and opened the car door for her. She slid in and her fingers ran over the leather interior, and she grimaced as he got in beside her. "Would you like me to pay for this? It's a top-end car—it looks expensive."

He frowned. "There's no need for that."

She wondered if she should remonstrate, point out the fact that she was an extremely wealthy woman. But his expression suggested the subject wasn't up for discussion.

As he backed the car out she noticed that, not only did the man who'd given them the car continue to watch them leave, but his assistants also stood to attention beside him, all eyes fixed on Rayan.

"They seem to know you," she said in a deliberately casual tone. Something was going on and she hadn't a clue what.

He shrugged "Ahmar is a small country."

"So small the border guards know you? So small the car hire guys know you?"

He didn't reply, and she decided that exiting the city through the crowded streets—over-run not just with cars but also carts and bicycles—was enough of an excuse to ignore her. She wouldn't push it—not yet, anyway.

They'd soon left the confusion of the city behind them and they were driving along a coast road with the brilliant blue sea to one side, and an unending desert to the right. Lauren hoped they'd keep beside the sea for a while yet. There was something menacing about the unknown desert. It challenged her—her knowledge about the world, and herself. She didn't know who she'd be in that desolate-looking place.

Much to her relief, they kept to the sea, ending up a few hours later in a town built around an almost perfect harbor, which protected an assortment of boats. But this was no Saint Tropez or Cannes. There were no luxury cruise liners here, only humble fishing boats. Her father would hate it, but Lauren fell in love at first sight.

She wound down the window to allow the warm sea breeze to take the place of the chill of the air conditioning. "What a beautiful place." Buildings clung to the cliff edge and tumbled down the steep roads which led to the picturesque harbor. But it wasn't either of these things which Lauren stared at. Dominating everything else with its presence was an ancient castle which sat at the harbor entrance, at the highest point of the town.

"Wow, that castle looks ancient."

He glanced at her. "We will stop here for a short time. There is something I need to do." But they didn't stop in the center of the town, they continued on up the hill to the castle. He swung the car around and parked in front of the door. She looked around, vaguely alarmed.

"Is it okay to park here?"

He glanced at her. "Yes."

He got out of the car without saying anything further. She'd known he wasn't a talkative man from the first moment she'd seen him, and she'd found it relaxing. But now she was beginning to think some communication might actually be helpful. Because with each mile she was leaving her own world behind and traveling into an unknown world of mystery, made still more mysterious by the inscrutable man beside her.

Her frown deepened as the huge wooden doors to the castle immediately opened and there were further greetings similar to the one at the car hire. She stood back and watched. These were more than casual acquaintances. Something was going on. Rayan turned to her and signaled for her to precede him into the castle. He switched to English.

"This is Lauren le Harivel," he said to the man who'd opened the door. "Miss le Harivel will be staying with me for a while."

"Welcome, Miss le Harivel. It is an honor to meet you. I hope you enjoy your stay in Ahmar.

"Thank you." She didn't add 'she was sure she would', because she was beginning to feel distinctly unsure.

However, that unsureness was instantly swept aside as she entered the magnificent hallway. Despite its age and scale, the castle interior appeared lived in and welcoming. Someone, or some family, had obviously made this place a home in the recent past. Maybe Rayan had grand friends who rented the place out.

Lauren followed Rayan to one of the imposing doorways and, without knocking, he opened it and walked through. Lauren followed him and felt her mouth open as she looked around the large room, which opened out onto a small terrace overlooking the harbor.

"Wow! What an amazing view."

He turned to her and grunted assent before entering an adjoining bedroom where she watched him rummage around in a wardrobe. "Good." He turned to her and held up some robes. "You'll need these. We'll go now."

She looked around in a panic, hoping no one would come in and find him riffling through their possessions.

"Rayan! You can't just come in here and take things!"

"Yes, I can." He put his arm around her to usher her out quickly.

"But you could be found, you could be seen. You could be arrested!" She had an idea that the armed guards she'd seen wouldn't treat a thief gently.

He huffed a laugh. "Nobody will arrest me, Lauren."

"Rayan! Give me one good reason why not."

He stopped and put his hands on her shoulders, and looked deep into her eyes. "Because this is my family home. These are *my* things. I own them."

"But—" She was stumped for words. How could she tell this man he was delusional? He was a horse-wrangler, a blacksmith, a stable-hand, not an owner of a castle. "But, Rayan, I don't understand."

"What is it you don't understand?"

She opened her hands wide. "I'm beginning to think there's nothing I *do* understand."

He smiled, took her hand and led her to the sideboard. He picked up a photo from the selection of ornately framed photographs clustered along its surface and held it out to her. "That's me. That's my family."

She took it from him. "You?" She peered closer at the boy, then looked at the other photos when he was older. "It *is* you."

"Yes, I think my mother—whose room this was—was the only person in my family who had photos of me. Of course that was before…" He trailed off. "Anyway, here." He held out the robes to her. "You'll need to wear these. What you are wearing is suitable for the city but not where we're going. Our people are more traditional there and it would offend them."

She blinked lightly, but realized she had no choice. She was in Rayan's hands now. She shrugged on the abaya and glanced in the mirror as he lifted a scarf over her head and showed her how to fix it.

She turned to him. "There, how do I look?"

She was rewarded with a warm smile. "Very satisfactory." He kissed her. "I will enjoy taking them off you again later. But now"—he stepped away—"it is time to go."

He took her hand and tugged her to follow him outside.

But she resisted. "Rayan. This place is beautiful. If this is your home, why don't we stay here?" She looked around with sudden longing at this small but beautiful castle. She suddenly didn't want to leave it and move into the unknown.

He looked at her strangely. "It might belong to me, but it's not where I live. It holds too many memories. My home is in the desert and that's where we will go." He squeezed her hand. "Aren't you interested in seeing where I live?"

"Yes, but—"

He silenced her by placing his finger against her lips. She remembered how he'd made love to her on their last night in England, and all doubts melted away. She couldn't wait to have him inside her again. "No buts. It's only a few more hours of traveling and then we'll be home." He pulled her into his arms and gave her a long, languorous kiss. "Okay?"

She nodded; she was incapable of doing anything else. But, as they drove away from the castle, with its soaring stone walls rising high above the lively harbor, Lauren couldn't help snatching a last look with regret.

And that regret only increased as they drove along a seemingly endless road which was hardly a road, across land which bore no resemblance to any land Lauren had ever known. And, with each passing mile, she became a little more nervous, a little more afraid, more dubious about the wisdom of her decision.

And yet, as her doubt grew, she sensed that, with each passing mile, Rayan relaxed a little more. It seemed the further from civilization they got, the happier he became. It was the opposite for her. She bit her lip as she surveyed the sandy, flat plains along which they drove. She could feel the tension sitting in the pit of her stomach like a low growl of anxiety, ready to bite her.

"There." Rayan pointed, and Lauren looked straight ahead but saw nothing to begin with. Rayan shot her a quick smile.

"That shimmer on the horizon, the slight cloud above it, that's where we're going."

"Um," she grunted, unable to think of any more appreciative response to the sight of a cloud.

But the cloud grew, took shape and color and, by the time they'd reached it, had turned into an oasis of greenness and unexpected civilization in an expanse of sand. After hours of nothingness, she felt a surge of excitement to arrive in such an exotic place. Towering palm trees—their feathered green blades contrasting starkly against the blue sky—sheltered a large lake with various dwellings and tents scattered around. It looked orderly, she thought, as she stepped out of the car and glanced up to see an ancient church, a remnant no doubt of Roman occupation. Orderly, unexpected, and strangely exciting.

"Welcome to my home." She joined him, looking out across the lake at the activity beside the houses. "It's nothing like you're used to. No doubt you hate it."

She listened to the tinkling sound of someone walking along with a tray of glasses, the wild cry of a hawk overhead, and the rustling of the protective palm trees providing shade in this stark landscape. She shook her head.

"And I'm sorry you don't like it," he continued, "but it's necessary."

"Rayan," she said, moving in front of him so he was forced to look at her. "How can you think I wouldn't like something like this? It's fabulous. *Literally*. I mean it's like I've stepped into one of the fables, the tales of my youth—Arabian nights or something." She grinned. "I know I'm going to find it hard to settle, but honestly, I'm excited."

She looked up into his eyes, trying to read them. Usually he was hard to read, but now there was a strange progression of emotions which shifted across his face. If she'd had to name them, she would have said there was initial relief, followed by confusion, followed by a spark of anger that was quickly seized and contained, returning his face to its usual fierce, but unreadable expression. What she didn't see was what she wanted to see—pleasure.

"Come, I will show you where we'll be staying."

He might not say much, and his face might not betray his feelings, but when he put his arm around her shoulder in both a gesture of ownership and a caring way, she felt reassured. She bumped against him as they walked up to a tent which was grander than any of the others and stood a little apart, with a cluster of stone buildings behind. He pulled aside the curtain which covered the entrance and stepped to one side to allow her to enter first.

"This is where I live."

She slipped off her shoes and stepped into a different world. The tent had obviously been well-tended during Rayan's absence. It smelled aired and clean. Unknown hands had polished the brass lamps and other fittings until they glowed in the dim light of the tent. The rugs underfoot weren't gritty, but plump and velvety. In the center of the tent was the bed. This tent obviously wasn't a place for sitting, for eating, for doing anything other than sleeping. But, from the luxurious look of the bed—the only piece of raised furniture in the tent—with its soft duvets covered in richly-colored silk, and the scattering of cushions, it appeared that that function was not under-estimated.

He cleared his throat as if he, too, was thinking about the bed. "There are washing facilities adjoining the tent."

She was relieved. It was one thing to live communally with people who spoke an unfamiliar language, ate different things, and, culturally and literally, were a thousand miles away from her life, but it was quite another to share their washing facilities. She was thankful for small mercies.

"You may change here. I must meet up with the men." He pointed to the village closer to the lake.

"Of course." But there was no 'of course' about it. She had no idea what she was meant to be doing, what she should change into, or why he had to meet up with the men. What about the women? And why did he *have* to meet them, anyway?

"And then maybe you should get in touch with your father? Let him know you're safe."

She shrugged. "There's no need for that. He won't worry."

"Why not? Doesn't he love you?"

She frowned. Rayan said so little that what he said was always important. Why did Rayan care if her father loved her?

She grimaced. "Yes, he loves me, and he needs me. But he will only truly understand that if I'm not around."

The tension around Rayan's mouth eased. Her answer seemed to satisfy him. She opened her mouth to ask him what difference it made to him whether or not her father loved her. But he turned and left the tent before she could gather her courage, shutting her off in this strange, exotic world. She slipped off the dusty abaya and sat on the enormous bed. Why was Rayan so concerned about whether or not her father loved her? She sighed. Maybe Rayan was simply relieved, because it was what she wanted. She liked that idea.

LAUREN TOOK her time getting dressed in the freshly laundered abaya that had been thoughtfully left for her on the bed. Then she lay on the bed, glad of the opportunity to stretch out, and waited for him to come to her. But after an hour he still hadn't appeared. She jumped up from the bed and paced the floor. This was ridiculous. She hadn't traveled over three thousand miles to remain in a tent! It was like being at home, secluded in her rooms in the manor, only venturing out onto the estate for work, or in the evening to walk in the peace and quiet once most of the workers had left. She refused to continue to be that shy, retiring woman.

She took a deep breath and stepped outside into the late afternoon sun, shaded by the overhead trees. She saw him immediately. He was seated on a rug drinking coffee, surrounded by men. They appeared to be deep in conversation. What made her hesitate was that all the men's eyes were on him, and he was talking, not in the short staccato sentences he used with her, but in a flowing stream of words and with an attitude which commanded attention. He looked like a different man.

Suddenly he looked up, their gazes clashed, and he barked a command at a woman who quickly made her way over to her.

"Come with me, Miss Le Harivel, and allow me to show you around," the woman said, in unexpectedly perfect English.

She cast a quick glance at Rayan, who had resumed his conversation and was no longer looking at her. She had so many questions to ask him, but they could wait until tonight. Because she knew that whatever happened during the day, he would be alone with her at night.

Rayan watched her leave with relief. The elders of the village would not dare question his motives or actions, but still he knew he had some explaining to do. And when he had told them what was going on, he knew it would only be a matter of time before word got back to Lauren. But he'd deal with that when it arose. Not before. She need not know that he'd caught her in a trap in order to avenge her father's treatment of his sister. Not immediately, anyway.

He closed his eyes briefly under the late afternoon sun, which penetrated the palm fronds and fell over the men in a dappled light. It was good to be back in his country. It was where he belonged. But he couldn't help comparing his feelings the last time he was here to what he felt now, being with Lauren. Yes, he'd succeeded in what he set out to do—snatch her from under her father's nose—but what he didn't understand was why he felt so conflicted.

LATER THAT NIGHT, Lauren lay in bed, her hands clutching the covers, as if she were the virgin she no longer was. She waited and listened to the songs and the sounds of the musical instruments die down, and knew that he wouldn't be able to delay coming to her bed much longer.

If he was hoping she'd be asleep, he was out of luck.

The evening had been an odd one. It had been spent mostly with the women who were friendly and curious. She'd also eaten dinner with them, seated outside the tents in the comfortable heat of the early evening. It seemed life was far more communal here than back at home. She hadn't talked to Rayan. He was seated far away from her and always appeared to be busy. Besides, she didn't need to make a scene, knowing that the night would come and he wouldn't be able to avoid her any longer.

Eventually, after the sounds of people talking and preparing for the night faded out, she saw the tent curtain shift. She watched as his dark shadow moved quietly around. She heard him undress and then get into bed. The bed was large and it would have been perfectly possible to lie, without touching, all night. But she had no intention of doing that.

She could hear his even breathing and could see his eyes

were open. It was as if he didn't know what to do. But she did.

Without a word, she rolled onto her side until her naked body was pressed against his. He snapped his head around and looked at her, his dark eyes and expression inscrutable in the near pitch darkness. He said nothing. Two could play at that game. At that moment, she didn't want answers, no matter what he might think. She wanted to vent her frustrations—both physical and mental—on him.

She placed her hand on his stomach and spread her fingers over the muscles which clenched under her touch. She moved lower and touched the tip of his erection. His hand slapped down on hers and he uttered a sound which could only have been called a growl.

"What are you doing?"

She refused to move her hand. "I'm touching your body. What do you think?" She could hear the thread of steel in her own voice and could see that he heard it, too.

She eased herself on top of him, allowing her peaked nipples to rub against his chest as she did so. Her face was close to his now. All she'd have to do was lower her mouth to his to find the sweetness she knew lay there. Instead, she licked her lips.

"And I'm going to make love to you," she breathed. Where she got the courage to say such a thing, she had no idea.

She placed her hands firmly on his shoulders, holding him in place. She knew he was far stronger than she was and could easily move, but he didn't. It seemed he liked, or wanted, what she was doing. It gave her a sense of power and control which had been missing from their relationship till now.

She pressed her lips against his, before running her tongue teasingly along his lips. Then she positioned herself over him, one leg on either side, her hands still firmly on his shoulders while she angled herself, and then rose and fell, allowing the tip of his cock to touch her clitoris.

She'd intended to tease him, but in the end it was she who could wait no longer. She took hold of him with both hands and eased herself onto him. She closed her eyes and gasped as she savored the slow slide of his body entering her. He reached out and played with her, enabling him to slip inside her. She threw her head back, her eyes still closed as he continued to use his clever fingers on her. But she didn't need them and with a guttural growl she opened her eyes, leaned forward and allowed her blonde hair to fall over her face and shoulders, its length tickling his chest as she rose up off him and then down again.

She watched him from under lowered lids. She had him this time. And she continued, slowly to begin with, but as her own needs became paramount she moved more quickly, more urgently.

With one swift movement he sat up, holding her close as she bounced up and down on him, needing to give herself pleasure. It came in an explosive flash, and she could feel her internal muscles caressing him, taking everything she could from him, holding him captive to her needs.

For one long moment they kissed, and she lay snuggled in his arms, but then the kiss deepened, and she noticed his arousal and she realized there would be little rest to be had that night.

# CHAPTER 5

Lauren was awakened by the sound of people praying. For a moment she wondered where she was, but, as her eyes became accustomed to the gray light of pre-dawn, she remembered with a start. The desert air was chilly, the sheets were coarse, and all around her the rugs and textiles which hung around the walls of the tent created a muted, shadowy world which was nothing like her old home.

Then she moved and was reminded that a certain part of her had been well used. She winced. After the night of love-making they'd had, she longed for a hot bath, but she didn't know if one was available here, in the middle of the desert.

She eased herself up on her elbows and looked around. There was no sign of Rayan; he must also be at prayer. She'd traveled all this way with him and hadn't even asked him about his religion. Of course he was Muslim. She swung her legs onto the woven rug which covered the floor, and winced and wriggled on the bed with the memories of last night's lovemaking still vivid. She touched herself and felt how sensitive she was, how primed she was for still more love-making. It seemed the more she made love with Rayan, the more she needed him. She sighed. She hadn't planned for this.

She pulled on her abaya for warmth and walked towards the rear of the tent, and opened a small tent flap which opened directly onto a covered passageway. She shivered briefly before stepping into a building which, from the outside, looked as if it had always been there but, inside, was deceptively modern. It housed the washing facilities, and the rear part was for their own personal use.

A quick glance revealed no baths, so she opened the door to the shower and turned it on. She was relieved to see hot water gush from the overhead rose. She pulled off her clothes and stepped under the hot shower with a sigh.

By the time she'd exited the shower and dried herself and her hair on the plump towels which she discovered neatly folded on a side table, the sounds of the camp had changed. From the murmur of prayers, interspersed with the muezzin's cry, there was now the sound of activity. The occasional shouts of men mingled with the laughter of children and the calls of women, suggesting the morning had begun in earnest. And, if she'd been in any doubt, the seductive smell of coffee and the mouth-watering fragrance of freshly made bread told her breakfast was ready.

Silently, she pulled back the tent's curtain to find Rayan pushing his fingers through his hair and pacing the floor with a sense of disquiet which sent a chill to her heart. For a moment, she watched him unobserved. He hadn't heard her enter, and she saw something in him she hadn't seen before—confusion.

She stepped inside the tent. "Good morning." It sounded like a very formal thing to say, given the circumstances, but his stance and expression invited nothing more intimate. She glanced at him, but he said nothing. So she went around tidying the tent. "I hope you slept well? I know I did.

Although, it was colder than I imagined. I had always thought the desert was—"

She halted suddenly as he touched her arm. "Lauren, why are you talking like that? What's the matter?"

She turned to him and shook her head with a smile. "What's the matter with me? Nothing." She folded her arms and turned to him defensively. "Unless you count the fact that I've left my home to travel with a man I barely know and that man is looking at me now with an expression which doesn't fill me with confidence."

He grunted softly and twisted his lips into a rueful expression. "I'm sorry. This situation is… unusual for me."

"It's not 'run of the mill' for me either." She grinned.

He shook his head and his eyes lightened into a smile, something which didn't register on his lips. He opened his arms. "Come here."

She didn't need telling twice and was immediately enveloped in his arms, breathing him in and feeling his body aroused and ready for her. She groaned and pressed herself against him, kissing the bare skin at his neck. He gripped her shoulders suddenly and pulled away.

"What is it, Rayan? What's wrong?" She searched his face for an answer, which it didn't give.

"We shouldn't have made love without contraception."

She shrugged. "I wasn't prepared the first time. And then, well, I knew it's not my fertile time of month. So…"

He shook his head. "It won't happen again. I'll send someone into the city to get some."

"You don't have any here?"

"No."

She frowned. "Then I don't understand. Why didn't you get some at the airport before we came here?"

He stepped away and didn't answer. The look of confusion returned. There was something going on which she couldn't put her finger on.

"There will be no more... intimacy, until then. I've decided."

"Maybe," she said. She knew she should wait, but she knew that in just a few days she'd changed from a prim English woman to a woman who was a slave to her sexual appetite. She wanted him, and she knew how she could make him forget his decision. And she intended to show him exactly who had the power here.

She placed her hands around his neck and pressed herself to him on tiptoes and kissed him. For a second she wasn't sure if she'd misjudged her powers of persuasion. Then she felt a sigh escape his body and his lips move over hers in a caress which had her moaning in his arms.

Suddenly, there was a cough from behind them. She could have ignored it, but Rayan looked around immediately. A man stood at the entrance to the tent, outlined by the growing lightness in the sky behind him.

Rayan spoke to him quickly in Arabic, and the man answered in a tone which surprised her. The man left, and Rayan pulled her hands from around him and dropped them to her side. He shook his head and walked away without a word. A sense of panic filled her as she suddenly realized how little she understood this man with whom she'd been so intimate, how little she understood of his, or now her, role in this desert community.

She bit her lip as she watched him go. She didn't want to sound needy but the trouble was, she *was* needy. She was in a strange country with a man she barely knew, and that man was leaving her behind. "Where are you going?"

He halted, the curtain flap in his hand as he looked out into the desert, its growing brightness filling the shadowy recesses of the tent. He glanced back at her. "I have work to do. I've been away too long."

The panic stayed, gripping her gut even tighter. "I don't even know what it is you do."

"Do?" He frowned. "I work for my people, of course."

"*For* them?" she repeated, needing clarity.

"Lauren, don't you understand? I am their sheikh. I manage our community's affairs, they come to me for help. I am their leader, in every sense."

She swallowed, her hands balling into agitated fists as she tried to accommodate this new image of Rayan. The clues had been there ever since they'd landed in this strange land. Earlier even, if she'd interpreted Rayan's imperious manner better. He'd never been subservient. Even when following orders, he seemed only to be doing so because he thought they were a good idea.

"You're the leader of the people in this desert oasis."

"Yes, and the leader of the harbor town, of the area all around here. The tribal leader."

"So, you're a member of the royal family then?"

His face hardened, as if she'd struck him. There was something in that look which made her realize he was hiding something else, something unrelated to her. Exactly how much was this man hiding from the world? The thought made her feel intense compassion for a man who, it appeared, had led a life similar to hers—in charge, but remote and lonely. But what else was there to know about him?

"So what were you..." She trailed off. There was so much she wanted to know about him. But the main thing she wanted to know was what the hell he'd been doing in England playing the role of stable-hand when he was the equivalent of the lord of the manor here, in the remote desert.

He strode back over to her and tilted her chin up so she had to look into his eyes. "So what was I? What is it you want to ask me?" His touch was gentle, but his eyes were challenging her to ask the question she most wanted to know the answer to.

She gathered her courage. "What were you doing in England, working in my stables?"

The silence lengthened and thickened between them. Then his eyes shifted with uncertainty, and she sucked in a breath as she waited for the explanation. But before she could get one, there was a shout from outside the tent.

He stepped away from her without a backward glance. "I must go." He walked to the door and then turned around to her. "We will be gone most of the day. Rest after your journey."

"But—" There was no point continuing, because he was gone with a swish of the curtain which blocked out the sand and heat and dryness of the desert, leaving her alone with her doubts and questions.

She grunted with frustration and grabbed her clothes to finish dressing. All the while her mind raced over the enigma that was the man who'd captured her heart and body. Her thoughts kept returning to that same question. Why had such a powerful man—a man who looked completely at home in his world in a way he'd never been in England—been working in her stables?

That he was an excellent horseman, she had known. But that he was a man of power in his country, she'd had no idea. He was an enigma. He had a beautiful castle by the sea that had belonged to his family, which as far as she could see now stood empty. And yet he refused to live there. Instead, he lived in the small community, far out in the desert. And she had no idea why. He was as evasive about his family as he was about the reasons for being in England. But if he didn't tell her what she wanted to know, she'd have to find out another way.

After she'd finished dressing, Lauren checked her appearance in the hand mirror to make sure she was wearing the scarf correctly. It was odd. She had always felt hidden in England and yet here, in this strange land, where her body and usual clothes were hidden behind her scarf and abaya, she actually felt more visible. She felt more alive, more a part of the world than she had ever felt before. And more determined to find out what the hell was going on with Rayan. Whether she was here only for a holiday, or longer, it didn't matter—she was going to find out more about him.

Although the sun was still low in the sky by the time she left the tent, the women were already hard at work. She glanced around, but there was no sign of the men. She knew there wouldn't be. She'd heard the horses' hooves gather speed as they'd left the oasis.

She walked over to where the women sat preparing food, building up the fire, and talking over coffee. The talk fizzled out as she approached. And all eyes were upon her.

She nodded. "*Sabah al-kheir,*" she said with a smile.

"Good morning," said the women in English.

"Oh!" She grinned broadly, feeling both relieved and humbled by the fact they spoke English. Her Arabic greeting was courtesy of a basic phrasebook Rayan had picked up for at the airport. Her language skills extended little beyond that. "I didn't realize..." She trailed off and gave an uncertain smile.

"That we speak English?" answered a woman of about her age with a smile. It was the woman who'd showed her around the day before. "Many can't, but our sheikh's mother was English and made sure English lessons were taught. She used to say that it took nothing from us, only added to our knowledge. And I lived at the nearby port until recently, so my English is a little more fluent than the others."

Some of the other women nodded and muttered in Arabic.

The woman smiled again and gestured to the other women with a bob of her head. "But not everyone took to it equally. My name is Salma."

"Lovely to meet you, Salma. I'm Lauren."

Salma laughed. "We know who you are."

"I guess it's pretty obvious."

"That you've taken the eye of our sheikh, yes."

Someone muttered words in Arabic, to which the other women laughed and Lauren blushed. She'd heard the word 'bed', and suspected that their night's activities were being referred to. Lauren's blush deepened.

She decided to change the subject. "May I help?" she asked, and mimed stirring the pot. The mime must have worked, for the women shifted along, allowing a space for her to sit, although they looked uncomfortable about it. She took the proffered spoon and copied the actions of the other woman, stirring the mixture in figures of eight to stop it from sticking to the pan as it simmered over the low fire.

Salma rose and poured a coffee for Lauren, holding it out to her with a smile. "Coffee?"

"Thank you." Lauren accepted the cup gratefully and took a sip of the hot liquid before continuing to stir the pot. She didn't want to ruin their dinner, or their opinion of her.

Slowly they began to talk amongst themselves again. She listened to the mellifluous words and chatter—little of which she understood—ebb and flow around her.

She began to understand the odd word, as the women relaxed in her company, and they were soon teaching her the names of common objects as she helped them prepare food for the day. Between her pigeon Arabic and their halting

English, she began to ask questions and find out a little more about their world and the enigma that was Rayan. She hoped by the end of the day, before he returned, she'd find out some clues that would unlock his secrets.

As Rayan galloped through the desert to a neighboring tribe with his men, instead of contemplating the meeting ahead and the petty complaints he had to hear, his thoughts were with Lauren.

On one hand, everything was going to plan. He'd accomplished the mission he'd set out to do. On the other hand, *nothing* was going to plan because he hadn't expected to have feelings for the daughter of the bastard who had ruined his sister's life.

He hadn't brought any contraception with him because he'd wanted her pregnant to avenge his sister. But now, after the last few nights, he found his hatred for this woman—his lust and thirst for revenge—had waned. He couldn't take her in his arms and make love to her without awakening feelings inside himself which he didn't know existed. The intimacy he'd shared with Lauren had been nothing about revenge, nothing about sexual taking, and all about making love. And he didn't know what the hell to do about it.

He delayed his return to the camp as long as possible. But, eventually, he'd run out of excuses and they rode into camp just as the sun was setting. He didn't know what he expected to see on his return, but it was nothing like the scene that greeted him.

Lauren was seated at the center of a group of women who were laughing and joking with each other as if they were old friends. She had a baby on her knee, and was feeding him gently and yet firmly with some food from a bowl while the other women looked on. He stopped in his tracks. He couldn't believe that this was the same woman—Lauren le Harivel, lady of the manor—transported to this domestic Bedouin setting. It was a setting which was as familiar to him as his own hand, but should have been totally foreign to her. And yet when he'd first run his eyes around the circle of women, he hadn't noticed her. With her head bent over the baby, and one of the other women's hand on her arm as they talked, she blended in as if she'd always lived there. It was only when she looked up and her blue eyes caught his gaze that he recognized her.

There was a gruff laughed beside him. "It looks like your lady is fitting in well here. Maybe you should take her for your wife after all." His cousin laughed as he hefted the saddle from his horse onto a fence post.

"I don't need a wife," muttered Rayan.

"Everyone man needs a wife, and it shows disrespect to lie with a woman who is not going to be your wife. That is wrong, Rayan. I thought our grandfather taught you better than that."

Rayan was annoyed with his cousin as he watched him walk away. But he knew why he was annoyed—his cousin was correct. Somewhere along the way, the hatred, whose seeds had been sown in him as a child and nurtured as an adolescent, had twisted him. And it had culminated in this act of revenge which would hurt this innocent woman—innocent no longer, because of him.

He had intended to sit with the men, as was usual. But the expression in Lauren's eyes and the pain in his heart halted him. But only briefly. He gritted his teeth and, looking straight past her, walked over to the men. It wasn't until much later, after dinner, after the day was finally drawing to a close, that he could resist no longer.

"Big of you to join me," she said with a glower.

He deserved the comment but couldn't help be amused by her uncharacteristic snarkiness.

"I was intrigued."

She shot him a dark look. "So intrigued you came nowhere near me."

He leaned in to her. "So intrigued that I sat somewhere where I could observe you better, see how you fitted into this strange world in which you've found yourself."

The dark look dissolved in an instant. "You observed me?" Her voice was husky. "And what did you observations lead you to conclude?"

"That you have a remarkable capacity to fit in." He swept his hand at the oasis. "None of this is familiar to you and yet here you are, making friends, holding babies, as if you were born to it."

Her expression saddened, and his heart contracted. She pursed her lips and looked away.

He reached out and placed his hand over hers, curling his fingers around her hand. "What is it?"

She turned to him suddenly and he saw tears in her eyes, glistening in the firelight. "Don't you understand?" She shook her head in disbelief. "It *is* what I was born to." She tapped her fist against her heart. "In here." She swallowed and looked into the fire. "From when I was very young I was always searching for someone I could love and who would love me back." She shrugged. "But it wasn't to be." She turned to him once more, and he could see by the determined lift of her chin that any trace of self-pity had gone. "I was born to be a mother, I was born to be a wife. It's what I've always wanted."

Her words struck at the heart of him. The charade of revenge had gone far enough. It could continue no more. He sat back, feeling a steeliness fill his nerves and the place where his heart was. "I cannot be that man, Lauren. I cannot be a husband. My place is with my people. That is all."

She rose and stood over him. "Then why am I here, Rayan? Have you truly no feelings for me? Because in there"—she pointed to their tent—"when there is no pretense between us, I believe you do. It's out here, in the world, that you put up barriers." She rose and took a step away. "And you will never find happiness with those barriers placed around your heart. Believe me."

He grunted. "Why should I believe you? What would you know about such matters? You wear your heart on your sleeve. You know nothing of barriers."

"Not my own, perhaps, because you're right. I love freely. But I know enough about other people's barriers. I know enough about what it is like to love, and not be loved in return. Certainly, enough to know that I will not allow that to happen to me again. Either you own your feelings, or I will leave."

Without waiting for his reply—maybe she knew by now that she was unlikely to receive one—she turned and disappeared into the darkness.

He kept his eyes on the place where she'd disappeared through the trees, on her way to their tent. She never stopped surprising him. There was he believing he'd have to give her the ultimatum to leave when, instead, she turned the tables on him, told him to shape up or she'd leave anyway.

He grunted, unable to stop his lips twisting into a wry smile, and rose slowly to return to his men. She never failed to surprise him, turning things on their head, unseating his expectations of her. He couldn't help but like that. What he didn't like was her analysis of his emotions. He'd never analyzed his emotions, and he didn't intend to start now.

And there was one other thing he didn't like… something which lingered in his mind, settling into a dull ache until long after she'd gone to bed, long after everyone else had also sought their tents. He didn't like she'd been hurt.

But, as the fire died down into low-burning embers, he realized it was something more than that. What he couldn't bear was that he was going to do exactly as her father had done to her—bring pain to that heart which she appeared unable to protect.

# CHAPTER 6

Lauren lay awake, as she had most of the night, looking up at the roof of the tent, counting the patterns, imagining the things which created the shadows in the moonlight, before the moon vanished and the chill gray light of dawn crept in.

Throughout the whole of the night she'd been alone, but it wasn't until now that she gave up. Rayan wasn't going to come to her. She'd pushed him too far. She'd hoped that she'd make him think. But it seemed she'd made him batten down the hatches and turn his back on her completely. It left her no choice.

She gave her scratchy, tired eyes a brief rub before she flung the bedclothes off and, shivering, slipped on her robe. She walked across the chill tent towards the bathroom, checking what she'd have to pack. It wasn't very much. She wouldn't take anything other than what she'd come with.

When she emerged from the bathroom, drying her hair, she nearly bumped into him.

"Rayan!" He reached out to steady her, but quickly withdrew his hand and moved away. He pushed his hands through his already disheveled hair.

"Good. I'm glad you up. You'll need to gather your things. We'll be leaving at first light."

Although she'd been expecting this, her heart stopped and gathered speed again. She swallowed. She stared at him, but he didn't turn to look at her. Instead, he strode over to the entrance. He hesitated. If he hadn't hesitated, she didn't think she'd have said anything.

"You can't do it, can you?"

He half-turned to her and she could see his profile rimmed in the gray light of the desert. "Do what?"

She strode over to him. "You can't sort out your emotions." She poked his arm with her index finger. "You, with all your machismo, all your strong, silent stuff." She poked him again, desperate for some kind of response. "You haven't got the courage to face up to your feelings." She went to poke him again, but this time he twisted around and caught her hand with his.

"Don't do that, Lauren."

"What?" She glared at him. "Poke you in the arm, or tell you the truth?"

His mouth formed one hard line. "Both."

She softened a little. "So you know I speak the truth."

For a moment she thought she'd gotten through to him. His lips softened and opened as if he were about to respond, and his eyes had a vulnerability about them, which she hadn't seen before. But he covered it in an instant. He dropped her hand by her side. "I'm sorry, Lauren. I'm not the man you thought I was, so I think it best to wind up your holiday now."

"My bags are packed."

"Good. The women are preparing breakfast. After we've eaten, we'll leave."

After he left, she hurled the towel across the tent. It caught on a brass bed post. She might have packed her bags, she might have intended to threaten to leave, but she'd had no intention of leaving this man who'd begun to mean so much to her.

LAUREN WAVED goodbye to the women she'd met so briefly and yet had formed such a bond with, especially Salma.

When she turned to face the front of the car, Rayan glanced at her with a frown.

"What?" she asked him, annoyed by the glance.

He shrugged as he changed gear and they drove out onto the desert road, heading toward the coast. "You appear to make friends easily."

She grunted and looked out the window. "I certainly thought I had with you. But it seems I was mistaken."

His hands gripped the steering wheel before releasing it again, as if he was willing himself to relax. Well, she wasn't interested in him relaxing.

"You appear to only want me for sex, and have no respect for me as a friend."

Again the grip and release on the steering wheel. "You are mistaken," he said in measured tones. "I *do* respect you. That is why we are leaving. It is me who made the mistake of bringing you to the desert in the first place. It was not right."

She was intrigued. "Not right? For whom wasn't it right? It felt pretty right for me—at first, anyway. Until you started to ignore me, that is. At night in bed, making love to you, it felt right."

"It was the wrong sort of right."

"What? What are you talking about?"

"I mean," he said with deliberate care, "in our culture, I

showed you disrespect. That was pointed out to me and I have seen the error of my ways."

"And what if I was fine with what happened? Hey? I'm a grown woman, Rayan, and I knew what I was getting into." She turned towards him and placed her hand on his thigh to watch his reaction. He closed his eyes briefly, as if her hand had scorched him. All to the good. He wanted her still, as much as she wanted him. She just had to make him see. "I'll need to stop at the next town." She knew full well that the next town was the harbor town with the castle. And she had no intention of going any further than that.

"What?" He turned to her. "Why?"

"The usual," she said.

"But—"

"Rayan," she said, in a placating tone. "I'm sorry, but I get car sick. I'll need to stop for a while to stem the queasiness."

"Okay," he said. "Okay," he said more gently. "We'll stop at the castle for a break. You can walk around, do whatever you need to do, and then we'll proceed to the city and the airport."

She gave a non-committal grunt. She wouldn't be moving any further than the castle. But a quick glance at Rayan showed he'd interpreted her grunt quite differently. She smiled to herself as the desert sands passed by. He might think he was in charge, but he hadn't the first notion of how stubborn and determined a quiet, shy Englishwoman could be.

Rayan had intended to by-pass the ancient port of Qaleat Albahr. There were too many memories which hurt—and they were the good ones. But he had no choice but to stop. He might be the type of monster who'd seduce a woman for revenge, but even a monster had his limits. And he was determined not to hurt Lauren any further. She didn't deserve it. It was he who deserved to be punished, and he was doing that by sending her away.

As the outline of the castle grew larger, so, too, did Rayan's dread. He couldn't face what lay inside. At the last minute, he turned and drove down to the port instead. He pulled up outside a café. All eyes turned to him. His car was known to people, as was he. He got out, acknowledged greetings from the café owner who'd emerged from inside, and went around to open the door for Lauren, who hadn't waited, but had already jumped out, her leather sandals slapping onto the hot pavement.

More people had gathered around and were watching them from neighboring shops and alleyways. He was keen to get inside the café.

"Lauren," he said quietly. She turned at his voice and he indicated the café. "Would you like something to drink?"

She looked toward the café and then back at him and smiled sweetly. "No, I'd prefer to walk." She turned her face to the harbor and took a deep breath of salty air. "After so much desert, it's nice to smell the sea again." She turned to him with something of an afterthought. "And I'm sure the fresh air will be more effective at taking away my queasiness, than a drink."

He shrugged and slammed her car door shut. They had to pass more cafés and shops from which people emerged, having heard the news that their sheikh was paying them a visit for the first time in years. He continued to greet them and was soon swamped by them.

Without thinking, he put his arm around Lauren to protect her from the crush while answering the questions with which he was bombarded from all sides. He made his excuses and pulled Lauren across the road to where a footpath ran alongside the harbor.

"Wow," said Lauren, as they hurried away. "You sure are popular."

He shrugged. "Apart from the brief stop a few days ago, I haven't been here in a long time."

"But you're their sheikh, right?"

He nodded. He didn't want this conversation to continue.

"Then how come you're rarely here?"

"Because my home is in the desert."

They took a few more steps, and then she stopped beside some stone steps that led to a jetty and turned to him. She didn't speak immediately, just looked at him with those beautiful blue eyes, eyes that withheld nothing of herself, and which were far too probing for comfort. He looked around, unable to meet that penetrating gaze.

"Let's keep walking."

He kept his eyes fixed on the bright horizon until they watered. But still she didn't speak, and he was forced to turn back to her. Her expression had softened, as if she'd found what she was looking for and understood it, which made him feel even more uncomfortable. She shook her head and bridged the space between them in two small strides. She placed her palms against his chest. He felt their warmth, as if she had x-ray hands which sought out the very heart of him.

"Rayan, please do me a favor?"

He nodded. Aside from believing he owed her the world now, he had no other option, because every part of him wanted to do Lauren a very big favor. "Name it."

She tilted her head to one side and looked up at him with such sweetness that he knew he wouldn't be able to deny her whatever it was she wanted. Some women would have made the same gesture and it would have been calculated, but with Lauren it was genuine.

"Can we stay here, please? Just for a few days." She glanced around, closing her eyes against the warm breeze.

He could see her pallor and the fine skin around her eyes. He yearned to touch her cheek, which looked like silk in the bright sunlight. When she re-opened her eyes, they held a sparkle he hadn't seen before. "Please? It's so beautiful here. It would be lovely to stay here a while."

He was nodding before his brain could form an answer. "Yes, if you'd like to." He cleared his throat. What was he doing? "It would give me some time to catch up with my people." He glanced behind him to the café, where people continued to gather and talk, pointing his way. "There are issues they wish sorted which, apparently, my advisors refuse to hear."

"Good." She lifted herself on tiptoes and for a moment he thought she was about to kiss him. Maybe she was, but remembered where she was just in time, because she rolled back down to her heels and smiled. "Thank you."

As THEY RETURNED to the car, Lauren thought she'd always remember that day, that moment, when she'd looked into Rayan's eyes and seen him clearly for the first time. Her man was hurting. She didn't know why, but somehow she felt that being here, in Qaleat Albahr, opened up something inside of him, and instinctively she wanted to stay there. She knew it would be the key to unlocking the pain, which he tried to hide from the world.

She'd asked for a few days, but she had no intention of staying only for a few days. She was in no rush to return to England; everything she was interested in was here—with, and in, Rayan.

Something had happened to him out there on the point. After he'd been unable to hold her gaze and had done a 360-degree turn, absorbing the castle, the sea, and the small town of Qaleat Albahr. When he'd turned back to her, she could see a chink in his armor had appeared. She intended to chip away at it further until there was nothing, no shield, no protective layer between them. It might take a few days, a few weeks, or a few months. She had no one waiting for her in England. Her estate manager was perfectly capable of running the estate in her absence. She could take her time. All she had to do was persuade Rayan that he had to take his time, too.

By the time night had settled around the castle, Lauren knew she'd made the right decision. The castle, while ancient, had been well cared for over the centuries and was a comfortable home. The desert had its surreal glamor but there was no doubt about it, this castle felt like home in a way the desert never would. She'd enjoyed her visit to the desert, but she knew she could never live there.

She'd hardly seen Rayan since they'd entered the castle. A woman who appeared to run the household immediately showed her to a guest bedroom. The last thing she'd seen of him was when she'd turned back on the stairwell to see Rayan disappear through a door which she knew from her last visit, led to the office.

After indulging herself in a long bath, she had a rest, and it was only in the late afternoon that she began to explore the castle.

She stepped out of her room, closed the door, and looked around. From its grandeur she knew that the main bedroom —Rayan's room—was the one with the ornate door in the position of prominence. She hesitated outside it, curious to look inside, but continued on. She hadn't heard anyone else climb the creaking staircase, and she imagined he'd still be out and about with his staff.

She went downstairs and entered the room to which

they'd come on their earlier visit. It felt like months ago, but she realized with a shock that it was only a week. But she felt like a changed woman. She stopped in front of the mirror and looked at her reflection. She even looked different.

She touched her cheek with her finger. Despite the different diet, or because of it, her cheeks looked fuller and her complexion glowed. She pushed back the scarf which she'd thrown over her head, revealing a head of blonde, glossy hair. Even her hair looked fuller. But then, she'd lost her hair ties and didn't pull it back into a severe ponytail anymore. Rayan said he loved her hair. He'd pressed his lips against it and nuzzled against her. Just the thought of what he did, and how it affected her, brought a flush to her cheeks —she looked up—and a sparkle to her eyes.

Loving Rayan had changed her. She stiffened as she replayed her thoughts in her head. She held her own gaze steady. "Loving Rayan," she repeated out loud this time. But there was no questioning tone in her voice, no doubt. She knew she loved him in her heart, her soul, and her body.

But, for whatever reason, Rayan refused to listen to his own heart. She felt, deep inside of herself, that he felt the same for her, despite the fact he said nothing, despite the fact he wanted her to leave.

"You look lost in thought." The door clicked closed behind her, and she turned around. "Or maybe just lost in your own reflection?"

Was it her imagination, or did he look less tense in these surroundings?

She smiled and turned her back to him, looking once more in the mirror. "I was just talking to myself," she said, aware of him closing the distance between them. She glanced above her head to where he now stood, looking not at himself, but at her. "Sometimes it's the only way to have a conversation."

His lips twitched, and he slipped his hands around her waist. "Are you accusing me of being a poor conversationalist?"

She raised an innocent eyebrow. "Poor? You can only be poor if you actually try something. I don't think you're familiar with the concept of conversation."

His lips fell back into his habitual hard line, and his brow lowered. "Is that right? Then, tell me, what is it I'm doing right now with you?"

She twisted in his arms to face him and his hands found a natural home around her bottom, which he caressed. She reached up and put her arms around his neck. Their hips bumped lightly together.

"What you're doing is mistaking conversation for foreplay."

He grunted with amusement, and his face lightened. He swept his lips across her forehead, breathing in her freshly washed hair. "Why are women always right?"

She shrugged. "It's just the way it is. You'll have to get used to it."

But she felt her own smile fade as his fell once more. It was frustrating, continually seeing glimpses of the real man behind the facade before the shutters fell.

She drew her finger around his face. "Rayan, tell me, what is it?"

"I can't allow myself to get used to it, Lauren. I can't get used to you being around, because you won't always be here."

She opened her mouth to speak, to deny his claims, to tell him she could always be around if only he accepted his feelings for her. But he placed his finger on her lips, silencing her. He wasn't ready to hear her. Not yet. But he would be.

She went on tiptoes and pressed her lips to his. She knew how to get through to him. She knew how good their bodies were together and how, when they made love, she could make him forget everything except the pleasure they found in each other.

And she did. Except when they made love, she found another barrier had been placed between them. Wherever Rayan had spent the afternoon, he'd returned with contraceptives which he insisted on using. She might not become pregnant as she'd come to hope, but there was time for that yet.

Rayan couldn't believe how sweetly the days passed. He'd only intended to stay for a few days to give Lauren the holiday she'd asked for. But each day had passed into another until now. As he counted the days on his computer, he realized a month had passed at Qaleat Albahr. A month in which he'd reconnected with his staff and with issues which he'd previously delegated. And, as he sat back and glanced outside the window at the sunset, having completed an afternoon of meetings and paperwork, he realized that he'd enjoyed the month. Not only being with Lauren—which continued to surprise and delight him—but reconnecting with people from his past. People who'd known him as a little boy, and his mother and, in some cases, his grandparents. He hadn't considered the effect it would have on him, but it seemed connecting with his people and his past had had a more powerful effect than he could have imagined.

He rose and went to the window. From his vantage point, he could see the stone balcony where he and Lauren sat in the evenings. She was there already. He smiled just to see her there. He could tell her mood from her movements. Tonight she looked a little agitated, which surprised him. Whatever she felt, she expressed, both in her face and in her body. She was like a light in his darkness, a joy in his pain. He knew he didn't deserve how happy he'd been this past month, because he was merely delaying the inevitable.

He'd managed to keep her as isolated from the outside world as possible by limiting internet and phone access. She'd accepted his word that such technology was emerging in this part of his country. It was a lie, but a necessary one. As soon as she made contact with her father, she'd know the truth. She'd know that their relationship was based on nothing but an act of revenge. But he had tonight, and he'd live it even though it might be his last.

As he left the library to go to her, he couldn't get out of his mind how much she'd hate him when she knew the truth, how she'd never be able to forgive him. But that would be his punishment for creating this mess.

When he stepped onto the terrace, Lauren was leaning on the stone balustrade overlooking the harbor.

She turned to him with a smile. "I don't think I'll ever tire of this view." She looked all around. "It's both exotic and homely, awe-inspiring and yet you feel it inside of you." She shrugged. "I don't know, it's kind of got to me." She turned and leaned against a pillar. The subtlety of her expression was shaded a little. "A bit like you."

He stood behind her, hands on her shoulders as he looked out at the view, more so that she couldn't scrutinize his own expression, which had grown more transparent with each passing day.

"Me? I've kind of got to you?"

She placed her hand on his and craned her neck to look up at him. "You know you have."

"And you, me. But that doesn't change things. You must return to your world, and me to mine."

She twisted in his arms. "But why, Rayan? If we feel the same about each other, why must we part?"

They were words she'd always skirted around in the past.

Maybe she also felt their days together were drawing to a close.

He opened his mouth to speak, but shook his head instead. His mind was a whirl of arguments and counter arguments, excuses and fears, and nothing emerged.

"Rayan, over the past days and weeks, I've seen you change. Here, in these surroundings, it's like the castle has opened you up a little. It holds secrets, I know, secrets which you won't tell me. But perhaps you should."

"Why?"

"Why?" She swallowed and looked nervous. "Because I've also changed since we've been here."

He narrowed his gaze on her, searching her face, trying to discern any changes. He shook his head. "In what way?"

"What if I said I wanted to stay?"

He shook his head instinctively. Then shook it again, more vigorously. "No, you can't. You must return to your home and no harm has been done."

"No harm? That's a curious way of expressing it. It's as if harm might have come to me. You didn't expect it to, did you?"

How could he answer that? Yes, he'd expected it to, because he'd planned it. He shook his head.

"Rayan. I have something to tell you."

He was distracted by the urgency in her voice. "What do you wish to tell me?"

"I guess there's no better way to tell you than to show you." She took hold of his hand and placed it against her stomach. "I'm pregnant."

"Pregnant?" he gasped, even as his hand felt her slightly rounded stomach. He sucked in a harsh breath. "You're pregnant? But..." But nothing. They'd made love enough times without taking any precautions for her to fall pregnant. He closed his eyes, unable to form a coherent thought. Part of him was appalled that his initial plan had worked so well, and yet another, far more powerful part of him was thrilled. Instinctively he'd wanted to give this woman, for whom he felt so much, his child. But how could he?

He took her chin in his hand, held her nervous gaze for a moment before taking her lips in a kiss in which he tried to convey everything because there were no words for how he felt.

Eventually, he pulled away and stepped back. He had to separate himself from her. He was scared she'd see right through him to the darkness that lay at the heart of him. But he had no choice but to continue. A baby changed everything.

"We will marry."

She laughed. "Is that your way of asking me?"

"Yes." For a moment he thought she might refuse. "You *will* marry me, won't you?"

Her eyes brimmed over with tears and she nodded. "Yes."

"Good. Stay here. I must get something."

He left her looking bewildered. He needed to make sure of things before he had a chance to change his mind.

He entered the drawing room, looked around, and his eyes lingered on his mother's jewelry case. He opened it and found what he was looking for. His mother had had to leave behind the engagement ring, with its large sapphire and diamonds, along with all her other possessions, when she'd fled to England. Here was something to show how he felt.

He paused in the doorway, with the ring pressing into his palm, and watched her. Eventually she would know what he'd done. But he was determined that they'd be married by then. Because only then would he stand a chance of her staying with him. And that was all he wanted now.

# CHAPTER 7

"Rayan! It's beautiful!" Lauren lifted the sapphire and diamond engagement ring into a stream of sunshine, and the light shattered into myriad pinpricks that made her face appear unearthly. Rayan held his breath, wondering if he'd done the right thing. Was it right to promise a future he couldn't give, a future she wouldn't want when she discovered the truth?

Then she moved the ring. The light shifted, and she smiled, her face now back to normal. He released his breath. The smile turned into a laugh, and she shook her head. "I can't believe it. I thought you'd run a mile when I told you. But, instead, you return with this."

Rayan frowned at her response. It was what he'd always intended to do, and he felt the sting of her accurate observation. He swept his fingers across her cheeks, wiping away the tears. "So, will you marry me?"

She laughed again, and her eyes misted with more tears. "Yes, of course, yes. I think I've loved you from the very first moment I saw you."

He smiled at the thought and pushed her hair from her

face and kissed her. "You," he said softly against her lips, "are confusing lust with love."

She shook her head. "It's all one to me. I'm in lust with you, and I'm in love with you. It's never happened before, and it'll never happen again. You're the only man for me, Rayan."

He felt at once deeply satisfied to have the woman who would be his wife, and mother to his child, say such things. But, at the same time, her words rang a bell of warning, which he immediately rejected. He knew how this would play out, and that, at some point in the future, he'd have to heed that warning. But not now. He pushed it to the back of his brain, where he kept the things he refused to think about.

"You are my woman now, Lauren." He held her tightly to his chest, raking his fingers through her beautiful blonde hair. "I feel you in every part of me, and that will never change." While she might talk of love, he couldn't. He was no connoisseur of love. He felt her at an elemental, visceral level, which nothing could alter—not time, not circumstances, not her feelings for him. He knew her feelings would change when she knew the truth, but his wouldn't.

She looked up at him with eyes so trusting they hurt. "You haven't used the word love."

"It's only a word, Lauren. What I'll do is show you how I feel." And without waiting for a reply, he lifted her into his arms. She gave a small yelp as she snuggled against him, and he kicked the door to the bedroom open and strode across to the bed. He stood her gently down, kissed her, and then stepped away, his fingers taking hold of her abaya and pulling it from her body. It fell to her feet. Then he turned his attention to the dress she wore. It was a sun dress, and he slid down the zip and pulled the straps from her shoulders. She wasn't wearing a bra, and he dipped his head and took each nipple into his mouth in turn, suckling lightly until he heard her moan. Only then did he pull away and push down her knickers. She stepped out of them obligingly. He raked his gaze down her body. Lauren had never looked more lovely. He wondered why he hadn't guessed before. There was a blooming quality, a lushness to her body which she hadn't had before. There were no longer any traces of the girl he'd once mistaken her for. She was all woman now.

"You are so beautiful."

He swept his hands over her stomach, hardly able to believe that a new life lay inside. His son. He shook his head, and his eyes watered. It was her turn to wipe away his tears.

As she kissed his closed eyelids, he could smell her scent and knew he couldn't wait any longer. He pulled off his clothes, lifted her into his arms, and then placed her gently on the bed. But, it seemed, she didn't want gentle.

She opened her legs wide for him and touched herself. Her eyelids fluttered, and she licked her swollen lips as she uttered the most sexual moan he'd ever heard. He immediately slid inside her. He could feel the grip of her hands on his shoulders and his back, urging him on. It was the first time in weeks that he'd made love without a condom, and he relished the immediacy of the sensation.

To begin with, he thrust carefully inside of her, his fingers skimming over her barely showing stomach. Then she dug her nails into his flesh.

"I'm not made of fine china, Rayan. Do what you usually do, please..."

He didn't need to be asked twice. This time he thrust into her, as she wanted him to, hesitating for a moment deep inside of her, making her aware of exactly how he filled her, before drawing out slowly and thrusting back quickly inside her. He built up the speed according to her response. He knew her now, knew how acute her need for him was, how aroused she became and when she wanted him to come inside her. He obliged, enjoying the feeling of pumping his seed deep inside of her. With a baby in her belly and his seed deep inside of her, he knew he couldn't ever let her go.

But, as he withdrew, he also knew that he'd have to come up with a plan fast.

He lay on the bed beside her and drew her into his arms, sweeping aside her hair and feeling her warm breath on his neck, her satiny smooth skin and delicate curves under his hands. How could he ever have thought he could use her and walk away? He could hardly remember the angry man he'd been when he'd traveled to England in search of the heiress in order to ruin her.

His fingers spread over her sex, playing with her until she was wriggling once more in his arms. Ruin? How could such bliss be ruin?

Much later, Rayan left Lauren dozing on the bed. His eyes lingered on her before he closed the door quietly and walked away. Whatever happened after Lauren discovered the truth, they'd be married. And then he might stand a chance of a future with her. But first, he needed to update his brothers—in person.

LAUREN WATCHED Rayan leave from beneath lowered lashes. He thought she was asleep, and she didn't tell him otherwise. He'd told her earlier that he would be away for the rest of the day. She knew better than to ask where he was going. Questions about his whereabouts, his past, his family, were always met with silence—with a closing down of his expression.

She'd spent the past weeks watching him, trying to understand him. But he wasn't an easy person to know. He kept secrets—how many she didn't know. But she knew they were rooted in his past.

Initially, she'd made the mistake of asking him. She'd

gotten nowhere with that. So she'd been forced to listen—not only to what he said, but what he didn't say, as well as to listen to his staff when they didn't think she was around. Sometimes it paid to be the kind of person people didn't notice. People other than Rayan, that is.

She smiled to herself as she thought of the way he'd always turn to her when she entered a room, even though she made no sound. Of how he'd look for her when she was curled up, out of sight in a chair. They had a connection that went beyond the physical and nothing, she knew, could change that.

But even with that connection, or perhaps because of it, she wanted to help him, because she understood that there was a part of him that was in pain. Something was holding him back, and she was determined to find out what it was. It was even more important now that she knew her future was with him.

She rolled onto her back, looking up at the shadows darting across the plain white ceiling, criss-crossed with ancient wooden beams, and grinned. It was what she'd always wanted—to be married to a man who only had eyes for her, and a baby… Many babies. She reached over and hugged a pillow as she allowed herself, for the first time, to imagine a future, the kind she'd used to fantasize about—now made real.

AFTER SHE'D SHOWERED and dressed, Lauren ventured downstairs into the kitchen to find Salma—the woman she'd met in the desert. Rayan had arranged for her to return to Qaleat Albahr to keep Lauren company when he was away. Usually Salma came to her, but this morning Lauren wanted to join Salma with the other staff.

She didn't know why, but Rayan preferred her to keep to

their part of the castle, and not mix with staff—maybe that was the old autocratic Bedouin ways. He hadn't given her a good reason, so now that he was gone, she immediately made her way there. She was sure that, whatever he was hiding, someone, somewhere, could shed light on it. Salma might be too discreet to let anything slip, but she hoped the housekeeper wouldn't.

Salma had gone out, but Lauren, with her increasing vocabulary and the housekeeper's rudimentary English, had soon persuaded the woman to join her in a cup of coffee. It had been something she hadn't the opportunity to do when Rayan was around. And it didn't take long before the housekeeper had relaxed and talked easily about the old days. It took only one question about Rayan's mother for the woman to open up about her.

Lauren forgot her coffee as she listened to the woman talk. It appeared that the only person who didn't adore Rayan's mother had been Rayan's father. It took only a few promptings to discover his identity, and then she set the coffee cup down on the saucer with a clatter.

"The king?" she asked incredulously. "Rayan's father was king?"

"Yes, of course." The old lady's brow furrowed in confusion. "Did you not know that?" She shrugged. "Perhaps our sheikh doesn't speak of it. The old king had no liking for family, other than the present king's mother." She pursed her lips and took a sip of the, by now, cold coffee. She bent her head to Lauren's. "The old king was a very hard man." She shook her head. "He could be a very… cruel man, especially to our sheikh and his mother."

Lauren pressed her hand to her head, which was beginning to throb. She tried to hide the confusion. She didn't want this woman to stop talking. Lauren forced herself to smile and took a measured sip of the cooling coffee. By the time she'd replaced the coffee cup onto its saucer, she'd decided a more indirect approach might prolong the conversation.

"And did you also work for the old king?"

"Oh, yes. I've always been in the royal household."

*Royal household,* Lauren repeated in her head. She'd had no idea.

"And did you like the old king?"

The woman pursed her lips. "I shouldn't say, given the man was half-mad. But, no, he was very mean to our sheikh's mother, and to our sheikh. He refused to marry her when he should, and he tore her away from her son."

"He separated them?"

"Yes. And for years he kept Sheikh Rayan hidden from the world. We heard only rumors, of course, that he was being kept in the desert. He was enslaved like a dog." The woman made as if to spit before remembering where she was.

"He was kept like a dog?" Lauren repeated incredulously, her hand pressed to her chest to ease the sharp pain which had thrust through her at the woman's words. She hoped it was a figure of speech.

"Worse than a dog. No one I know would treat their dogs like the old king treated Rayan. Beatings, rationed food..." The woman leaned in. "I even heard he was chained in a cave for weeks at a time for being insolent. It was inhuman what he had to undergo."

"But why? I don't understand why. He was his son. How could he have treated him like that?"

"People say it was because Rayan's mother thwarted the king by escaping. But if she hadn't escaped, she would have been dead."

"So how did Rayan come to be in England with his mother?"

"She came and got him. Risked her life to get him out of

the country. There are rumors that a member of the royal family helped her. We don't know who. We didn't see him again until years later, after the old king died."

Lauren leaned back against the hard-backed wooden chair, drained. "That's so terrible." Her whole being ached in sympathy with what Rayan had had to endure at the hands of his father. "It must have had a lasting effect."

"Of course," said the woman quietly. "Of course." She petted Lauren's hand, as if she'd forgotten to whom she was speaking. "He was turned into a hard man because of what he endured. But he is fair." The woman smiled at Lauren. "And he is in love with you. That much is clear to everyone. We have never seen our sheikh here at Qaleat Albahr so much, nor have we seen him so happy."

Lauren widened her eyes in surprise. To her, Rayan didn't appear happy. He appeared contained, defensive, and it was only in their most intimate moments she knew he was… something, but happy wasn't the word she would use to describe him. Again, it underlined how little she really knew him.

"So," said Lauren. "The present king, Rayan's half-brother—"

The woman shrugged. "The three of them are like full brothers. Half-brothers, strictly speaking. It was the same with Madaniya, their sister. God rest her soul." She sighed. "Anyway, the three brothers rule this country of ours. Our new king has handed over governance of two-thirds of the country to Sheikh Rayan and Sheikh Adam. No doubt that is why he had to go there in such a hurry. Politics." She shrugged. "Of course, the king is in ultimate control of the country but he has wisdom which their father did not." The housekeeper sighed, looked into her cold coffee, and then jumped up. "I should go. I've spoken too much."

Lauren rose too. "Not at all. I've enjoyed our chat."

The woman smiled. "Me, too. The castle has been different since you arrived." She pressed her lips together as if she hadn't meant to speak. She gave a cursory bow, as if only just remembering Lauren's status, and then disappeared.

Lauren shook her head and watched the other woman leave. It seemed she was the only person in the country who didn't know Rayan's relationship to the king. She was pregnant with his child, engaged to marry him and yet she didn't know the first thing about him.

She felt a flicker of unease but firmly dismissed it.

She also hadn't known where Rayan was going to. And then there was the name of their sister. Lauren wondered if the name was a common one in Ahmar. Because it was the same name as the woman her father had had a brief affair with. And she'd been from Ahmar, as well. She frowned at the coincidence, then dismissed it.

Lauren grunted in confusion. Talking with the housekeeper had raised more questions than it had supplied answers.

RAYAN STRODE into the boardroom where his two half-brothers were seated, waiting for him.

Sheikh Zeeshan ibn Mohammed Aziz, King of Ahmar, looked up with a cool stare. Rayan didn't know how he always maintained such a coolness.

"Well, this is a surprise," Sheikh Adam ibn Mohammed Aziz said in an ironic tone. "We thought you were with Lauren le Harivel, in the desert, exacting revenge. What's happened?"

Rayan accepted a cup of coffee from the maid and waited for her to disappear. Then he knocked it back in one, needing its harsh strength to counteract the tiredness of the drive.

"She's pregnant," he muttered.

Adam's eyebrow shot up. "She's pregnant? That was quick, brother. I see you didn't shirk your duty." He nodded slowly. "Well done. You've done to the old man what he did to our sister. Except for one last step. And that is to leave her."

Rayan felt sick to his stomach. He rubbed his eyes, gritty with sand from the journey and tiredness. But that didn't explain their watering.

He shook his head, sat down, and put his head in his hands. Suddenly he felt the touch of his elder brother's hand on his shoulder. "What is it? What's the matter, Rayan?" All he could do was shake his head. Zeeshan's grip tightened on his shoulder. "I was always worried about this plan. The old ways of revenge are not always the best. Tell us what's happened."

"Rubbish," said Adam. "The old ways are still the best. They are old and established for a reason—they work. Your next step is clear. You do as le Harivel did to our sister. Remember our sister. She is dead because of him. He needs to be punished. He needs to be shown that he cannot do such a thing to one of our family and get away with it. You must leave her exactly as her father left our sister. *That* is how it works."

Rayan looked up at his two half-brothers. His elder brother, Zeeshan, was always the gentler, more thoughtful one, and Adam, the youngest of the three, always far harder. "The problem is that I have..." He hesitated as he tried to figure out words to express the inexpressible. "*Feelings* for her." He nearly choked on the word 'feelings'.

Zeeshan swiftly withdrew his hands, while Adam grunted in an exasperated way.

"What do you mean, feelings?" asked Zeeshan. "You *never* have feelings."

"Well, it looks like our tough brother has developed some this time," said Adam. "You picked a great time to do that, Rayan!" he said, with a shake of his head.

Rayan jumped up and walked away from his brothers, unable to take their scrutiny any longer. Zeeshan was right. He had never shown an ounce of emotion before, so why now? Immediately the vision of Lauren's face appeared in his mind and refused to shift. He knew the answer. It was her. It was all about her. He was powerless to prevent these feelings from emerging. He didn't even know he *had* any ability to feel them, not after what he'd been through.

"Now is not the time for regrets," said Adam. "Now is the time to finish the thing." Adam's hand grasped the air as if it were a throat to be crushed. Rayan's gaze was fixed on his brother's fist, around some phantom neck. Except it didn't belong to a phantom, it belonged to Lauren.

"Perhaps our plan of revenge should be abandoned," said Zeeshan. "If you have feelings for this woman, then maybe you should accept them. After all, it is something rare for you to show feelings."

Adam thumped the table with his fist. "Our plan must *not* be abandoned. We will look weak. Not only to her father, but to our people. Her death has leaked out into the public and become common gossip. We cannot risk being seen as weak by anybody. Where will it end?"

"Maybe it will end with understanding and peace," said Zeeshan.

Adam muttered the sort of expletives which Zeeshan would never normally allow. The tension increased as the two brothers bounced arguments back and forth, leaving Rayan stuck in the middle, confounded by the situation he'd put himself in, confounded by his feelings for Lauren. Slowly, he rose and came to his brothers.

"Stop arguing. There is nothing I can do, except stop this now. I started out for revenge. I'd dreamed of revenge, and that dream has become a reality. But it's a reality which has turned out to be a nightmare." He shook his head.

"So what are you going to do about it?"

He shook his head. "She's carrying my child. What do you think I will do? I've asked her to marry me."

Adam swore once more. Rayan ignored him.

"And what was her answer?" asked Zeeshan.

"Yes, of course," spat out Adam. "She's a le Harivel. She knows the value of marrying someone of Rayan's standing."

"All she knows is that I am sheikh of Qaleat Albahr and the surrounding area. She knows nothing of my family, nothing about the identity of my father."

"I don't believe it. She's as money-grabbing as all the others."

"Your idea of women is warped, to say the least, brother," said Zeeshan.

"Lauren is innocent in all of this. We will marry. I have no other choice now she is pregnant. I mustn't lose my son."

"Or daughter," said Zeeshan.

Adam dismissed their words with a sweep of his arms. "None of this is relevant. Marriage or not, it will not last—it *cannot* last. Once Lauren finds out why you came after her in the first place, she will leave."

Rayan had nothing to say to that, because it was exactly what he feared.

Zeeshan once more reached out to him, his eyes kind and wise. And not for the first time, Rayan saw his grandfather's eyes reflected back at him.

"We do not know that for sure. Let's hope Lauren is more understanding than you, brother," Zeeshan said to Adam.

"She'll leave. Why would she stay with someone she can't trust? Who would?" Adam glared from one brother to the other, then scooped up his phone from the table. "I'm going. I'll leave you two to it."

Rayan watched Adam leave with a bang of the door. He'd always been on the same page as his younger brother before. They were both angry people, who saw things in a more black and white way than their elder brother, the king. He realized with a shock, that he had, truly, changed.

Rayan rubbed his eyes. "Adam is right. As soon as she discovers the truth, she'll leave." He jumped up, twisted around, as if trying to find another way to interpret the future, but he didn't succeed.

"You're wrong, Rayan. There is a way."

"Tell me what it is, because I have no idea."

"Show her your *real* self. Tell her what happened to you all those years ago. Once someone understands something, then they are on their way to forgiving them. And Lauren sounds as if she's a thoughtful woman. It's worth a chance. Tell her."

Rayan shook his head. "She will never forgive me. She is a vulnerable, gentle woman who has given me everything in trust. And I have betrayed that trust. That is the one thing she will never forgive." He looked grimly out into the distance beyond the city, beyond the hills, to the port city where Lauren would now be waking, in a world which was not hers, trusting a man who she shouldn't have trusted. Vulnerable and alone.

# CHAPTER 8

"Rayan!"

Rayan slammed the car door closed and looked up to see Lauren running down the castle steps towards him. She glanced around and, seeing no one watching, ran into his arms. He laughed and swung her around. As the sun shone on the two of them, here in the place he'd always regarded as home—that was both wonderful and painful at the same time—he thought he'd never been so happy.

She reached up and cupped his face with her hands and kissed him. "What's happened?" she asked. "You seem different."

He put his arm around her shoulders and began to walk inside the castle.

"Nothing's happened. I just had to leave on an errand."

Was it his imagination or did Lauren look away too quickly?

"Well," she replied, "whatever the errand was, you seem pleased to see me."

He closed the door and once safely inside, away from

prying eyes, he gave her the kind of kiss which showed her exactly how pleased he was to see her.

"Um," said Lauren, when they eventually parted, licking her lips. "That was nice. I wonder if there's any more where that came from?"

"What have you done with my demure little English girl?"

She raised a suggestive eyebrow. "You've made her a woman, Rayan. And, I'm afraid, you'll have to live with the consequences."

This time he didn't bother looking around. He didn't care who saw him pick her up in his arms and walk up the stairs. She tried to wriggle out of his arms when they reached the top of the stairs, but her wriggling ceased and turned into a moan as his hand crept under her abaya, under the dress she wore beneath, under her underwear and found its wet target.

"Now," he said, "be quiet, because there are things I wish to do with you."

Much later, after he'd enjoyed lovemaking more profound, more emotional than he'd ever before experienced, Rayan stroked her hair as she nestled up to him, and realized that Lauren had been correct. He was different.

She'd been as responsive as ever to his touch. And he'd taken his time caressing Lauren's body and listening to her breathing, tasting her arousal, before giving her the ultimate bliss they both craved. And now, as she lay in his arms, he realized that their lovemaking had only been a temporary distraction from the truth.

Something had shifted inside of him. He felt more at ease with his feelings for Lauren than before. Now that he and his brothers had agreed that there would be no revenge, nothing to hurt Lauren further than he had already, he could enjoy her… for what little time he might have left with her, anyway.

But what if he could prolong his time with Lauren? What

if he could make her understand why he'd set out to ruin her? He closed his eyes in defeat at the very thought of it. How could he? His younger brother, Adam, certainly didn't think he could. Adam had been predictably hard—he was even more angry and bitter than Rayan was about the past.

But Zeeshan had thought he could do something. Zeeshan—whose kindness as a boy had eased his suffering; Zeeshan—who'd saved him from the streets of London and given him back his pride; Zeeshan—his brother. If there was one man in this world he trusted, it was him. And Zeeshan had told him to make himself vulnerable. Now, how on earth was he going to do that?

He cleared his throat. First, tell her where he'd been and who with.

"I went to the city today."

She shifted to look at him and gave him an innocent smile. "I know."

"Oh?"

"Yes, I know you went to the palace."

He raised his eyebrows in surprise. "How do you know?"

She traced her finger around his chest muscles. "I can't tell you that." She bit her lip, as if suddenly aware she might get someone into trouble. She was right, she would.

He grunted with annoyance. "I suppose this unknown person also told you who I was going to see."

"Yes, your brothers." She kneeled either side of his hips and sat down lightly on his knees. "Just as well someone told me." She leaned over him and kissed him. If she'd kissed him to distract him, it had worked. "If I waited for information from you, I'd never find out anything." She kissed him again.

For a moment, his distraction deepened as she swept her tongue up his body, grazing her peaked nipples against his chest. Then she sat back and looked at him.

"Seriously, Rayan, it concerns me. I'm pregnant with your

child, we're engaged to be married, and yet I don't know the first thing about you."

He was drawn back into the present with a smack. He gave himself a few minutes to bite back the first thing that came to mind—that he didn't want anyone to know the first thing, *or* the second thing, about him.

He bought more time by taking her hands and kissing each one in turn. "I'm sorry. I have a past which I find it hard to talk about. Ask me questions and I'll do my best to answer."

She looked down at his body and traced her finger along his scars. "Let's start here, with the scars. There's a story to tell here."

"Just one?" he asked, playing for time.

She stopped stroking him and looked into his eyes. He wondered if she knew. He knew her father had been trying to contact her, trying to track her down, but he'd made sure he couldn't find her. Or so he'd thought.

Then she sighed and shook her head. "Rayan, please, let me in."

Relief flooded him—it was clear she still didn't know. She wouldn't want to be let in if she knew how he'd begun this whole thing—with vengeance in his mind and in his heart—she'd want to run a mile.

He took her hand, which still lingered on his scars, and kissed her fingers, buying yet more time as he threaded his fingers through hers. He folded his hand over hers and looked directly into her eyes.

"I can't tell you while you sit naked on me. Go, get dressed, and I'll meet you outside."

"It'll be dark soon."

"So much the better."

He'd been thinking about the best way to make himself vulnerable, as Zeeshan had suggested. It was easier to agree than to do it. He'd spent his whole life doing the opposite. It went against everything he knew, every impulse that he had to defend himself. But instinctively he knew Zeeshan was right. He had to open up to Lauren. He had to be vulnerable for her—it was the only thing he could think of which might stop her from leaving him once she knew the truth.

And, as he watched her pull on her robe and walk over to the bathroom, he was glad they'd be outside as the brief twilight fell. He might have to be vulnerable, but it would be a lot easier if no one—especially not Lauren—could see his face as he told her some, definitely not all, of his secrets.

LAUREN EMERGED FROM HER SHOWER, dressed in one of the finest robes she'd found in the castle wardrobes. It was of silk and flowed around her like air—perfect for such a beautiful evening.

She checked herself in the mirror before leaving and was surprised. She looked a different person to the one she'd left behind in England, and it confirmed she'd done the right thing. She'd left behind a girl, and looking back at her now was the image of a woman, flushed from the shower, her features softly rounded. She touched her lips, which were still slightly swollen from Rayan's kisses, and smiled, looking up into her eyes which flared with desire at the thought of the man she was going to marry. And tonight she was going to take a step closer to him, unlock his secrets so she could know and love him even more.

Lauren stepped out of the doors onto the stone balcony, which overlooked the port. A welcome breeze blew across the facade of the castle, catching her hair, which hung loosely around her shoulders. She wore no scarf tonight, not when there were just the two of them.

He stood looking out across the bay toward the setting

sun and the desert. There was a tension in his shoulders, and in his hands, which gripped the balustrade as if for strength. The Rayan she knew never needed strength. If there was one thing she was certain about, it was that her man was strong enough to take on the world. Too strong, if anything. He turned toward her, even though she made no sound, and she met his intense gaze with an uncertain smile.

She walked over to him but stopped short as she noted he made no move to embrace her. Her smile slipped a little more.

"Rayan? Are you all right?"

He gave a brief nod. He stepped away from the balustrade and gestured to the table, laden with food. "I thought you might be hungry after jumping on me as soon as I returned." His grin also returned. "Not to mention the fact that you're eating for two now."

She released a sigh of relief. He'd obviously pushed whatever he'd been brooding on to the back of his mind.

"You"—she tapped his chest—"are getting to know me." Unable to stop herself, she shifted her fingertips to caress the dark skin and hairs on his chest which peeped out from the white linen of his shirt.

He pressed his hand against hers. "And you, Lauren, are not so hard to get to know."

Her smile faded. She felt hurt by his statement, no matter how true it was. "I was raised to tell the truth, and I'm so used to my own company that when I'm with others, I say whatever I'm thinking. Is that so bad?"

He frowned and shook his head. "No, not at all. It's refreshing, it's lovely, it's one of the things about you I…" He trailed off and her hurt was compounded by the fact that he didn't utter the word she longed to hear from his lips. She couldn't bear seeing the barrier slam down over his features. A few moments ago they'd been expressive and warm. Now they'd grown immobile and cold. Wouldn't she ever get through to him?

"But you're right. I *am* hungry." She turned away, picked up some finger food off the table and sat in one of the chairs overlooking the sunset. He sat across the table from her, taking a sip from his drink. "And I'm also hungry for information, Rayan," she added softly.

He avoided her gaze and nodded. "You must excuse me. I find this very hard. I rarely speak of what I'm about to tell you. But my brother, King Zeeshan, suggested I confide in you."

"Why?"

Rayan twisted his lips, as if unwilling to state his first thought. "It does not matter. What matters is that I will tell you a little about myself so that you will understand some of the mistakes I make, the sort of man I am."

She gave an uncomfortable laugh. "What mistakes are these?"

He shrugged. "Everyone makes mistakes, don't they?"

"Yes, I guess, but it sounded like you must have made some big ones."

"That's true. I have. But I'd prefer not to dwell on them. I'd prefer to defend myself first by describing the things which affected me growing up. It's just… I don't know how or where to start. There is so much I have tried to forget."

"Begin by telling me of something you've tried but been unable to forget. What was your earliest memory?"

"Oh, that is easy. It's shame and regret at not defending my mother from the blows of my father."

"Your father beat your mother?"

"He was a monster. I don't know why. My grandparents were good people. No doubt the things he took made him worse than he already was."

"Like?"

"Drugs, drink, you name it, he took it and then he dealt with his anger by inflicting it on those around him, principally my mother and me."

She squeezed his arm. "I'm so sorry. No one should have to undergo such things. How old were you at the time?"

He shrugged. "I don't know. Young, five maybe. She only hung around for me and life for her got worse and worse until one day she couldn't take it anymore and smuggled me out to the border. But someone must have betrayed her. She was forced out of the country and I was kept behind. It remained that way for years."

She forced herself to break the silence, knowing a little of what had followed, but she didn't want him to know she knew. "What happened next?"

He sucked in a breath and met her gaze as if dragged back from his memories all those years ago. "Next? Oh, my mother told me afterwards that she spent years trying to get me back by official means but was always blocked, always told that her son would be much better off being raised the son—albeit illegitimate son—of an all-powerful king. And so she backed off for a few years until she heard the rumors."

There was something in the way he said the word 'rumors' which made Lauren's heart clench. She felt nauseous, hardly daring to break the silence. "What rumors?"

He looked at her with a heart-breaking directness she'd never seen before in his eyes. "About how he'd been keeping me. He'd moved me out to the out-house after my mother left, forbad anyone to call me by my name. I was always to be called *kalb,* or hound, even by the servants." He looked away again and squinted into the dying sun. "And I was kept like one, too. I was tied up and kenneled. My food was thrown at me—*when* it came. And I was beaten when I showed any emotion."

Lauren thought her head and heart would burst. She

stood up, let out a loud wail and, with tears running down her face, kneeled in front of the man who'd been taught not to show any emotion and rested her sobbing head in his lap.

He placed his hand on her head. "It's okay, Lauren. It was a long time ago."

She looked up at him through her tears and marveled that, after such dehumanizing experiences, he could be anything like normal. "I can't believe someone could do such a thing to another person, let alone a child." Just the thought of it made her cry harder, one hand placed on his leg, the other on her stomach where a new life lay, a life that she couldn't bear to think of would ever suffer what his or her father had. "How long did it go on for?"

He shrugged. "A couple of years. I would have been lost if it hadn't been for my elder brother, Zeeshan. He didn't even know I was in the compound until he overheard some servants talking and went looking for me."

"Did he release you?"

"He tried. But received his first beating for it. It laid him up for months but during that time he managed to get word to my mother and help me escape to her."

"Thank God for Zeeshan." In that moment, Lauren knew she'd always do whatever she could to help Rayan's elder brother.

"Yes. He's a good man and I owe my life to him."

"And so you eventually escaped and were re-united with your mother."

"Yes. I was taken overland across the mountains to a port where my mother was waiting and we traveled to England."

"Thank goodness. Please tell me that your life was good in England. I don't think I could bear it if it wasn't."

He didn't answer immediately, and her heart sank. He stroked her hair. "You are a good woman, Lauren, and you do not understand the evil and troubles of others, and I am happy you don't. It's nice to know that there are some people untouched by the miseries of this world."

"But what happened next, Rayan? Good or bad, I need to know."

"We moved around. You see, we both knew that my father would never let either of us go. We both knew that he would look for us, hunt us down, for the rest of his life. And so we changed our name and kept on moving."

"But at least your life had to have been better than it was before."

"Yes, but you must understand, I was damaged, mentally and physically." He twisted his arm in the dying light, showing the silvered scars which criss-crossed his arm. "But"—he lowered his arm and placed it around her shoulders, her cheek now pressed against his thigh—"my mother was even worse. She lasted only a few years and that only through sheer will-power."

"And then?" she whispered, not wanting to know what happened next but needing to.

"And then I went onto the streets. It was either that or be caught and returned to my father, and I was never letting that happen to me. I did what I had to do to survive."

"Like what?"

"Anything and everything. It's best you don't know the details. I was hardened already from what I had to endure at the hands of my father. Three years on the streets made me harder still."

She sighed, swept away the tears from her cheeks and blinked, trying to focus on anything but the pain she felt in every fiber of her being for the boy that was Rayan.

"When did it stop? What happened to get you out of there?"

"Zeeshan. My brother. As soon as our father died, he set about looking for me." He gave a gruff laugh. "It wasn't that hard. A dark-skinned boy on the streets who was good at fighting and who was known to the police. He found me and he brought me back to Ahmar."

"Thank goodness he did."

"He saved my life. No, what he did was to *give* me a life. He gave me the help I needed to fit in and he gave me purpose, as well as my lands. I owe him everything."

"He sounds wonderful."

"He is that and more, but what he couldn't do was take my anger from me. I managed to hide it well, but it burned inside of me." He turned to her. "Until you. You changed everything."

She quietened, wondering if she'd heard right. She lifted her head from his lap.

He smiled at her. "You've changed me. I don't know what you did, but I don't feel such bone-deep anger anymore."

"Oh," she exhaled, "I'm so glad. I couldn't bear to think that you continued to hold all that pain inside of you."

"It's still there, and I'm a hard man because of it. But I can tell you one thing, from now on, I will always put you first, no matter what you might think, no matter what you might believe of me."

She frowned for a moment and cocked her head to one side, trying to figure out exactly what he meant. "No matter what I might believe of you?" she repeated with an uncertain laugh. "Why would I believe anything bad of you?"

"Because I've done things I thought were right at the time, but which now, I realize, were far from right. I can see that now." He gripped her hands so tightly it hurt. "You must believe me."

"I do."

"Swear to God that you believe me."

"I don't need to. You can take my word for it."

"Please, just do it."

"I swear to God that I believe you." She swept her hand around his face, puzzled by his sudden intensity. "How could I not?"

He searched her face and then relaxed, as if reassured by what he saw there.

She sat on his lap then and kissed him, wanting to show him with more than just words how she felt about him.

"It's okay, Rayan, it's really okay. No matter what happened to you, your future, our future"—she raised his hand to her stomach—"will be wonderful. You can forget the past now."

He smiled briefly, but she could still see fear etched in his eyes. And she wondered if she'd ever be able to rid him of it.

"Trouble is, Lauren, I can't forget the past. My biggest regret is that my choices have made me more like my father than I care to admit."

"I think you have just admitted it," she said softly. "And that's a beginning. A new beginning from which we can both move forward."

She pressed her lips to his, willing him to respond, to forget the past and grab the present greedily with both hands. Then his mouth opened with a sigh and she twisted around and kissed him, with all the hunger she felt for him.

Everything was all going to be all right. She'd make sure it was.

# CHAPTER 9

The day began like any other of the previous two months. Rayan was gone from her bed before she'd awoken, still sunk into a deep and comforting sleep, her body satisfied from their lovemaking and her mind at peace for the first time in her life.

She always awoke as soon as he'd left the room, somehow aware of his absence. She rolled onto her back, her hands fingering her rounded stomach, and remembered with a joyful start why this morning was different to the others. Today, she thought, swinging her legs onto the rug and standing up and stretching, was her wedding day.

There was only one thing she was sad about. Despite having sent letter after letter, she hadn't heard from her father, or anyone from the estate, come to that. Her father was a technophobe and refused to use a computer, and what she had to say couldn't be read out by one of his glamorous temporary secretaries. So she'd resorted to snail mail. Not that she had much choice. Whenever she'd asked Rayan for wifi access, he'd always swept away her questions with some excuse or other—the country's telecommunications weren't advanced in that region, there was some kind of cabling issue, the hardware was about to be updated. Whatever the problem was, it had become her problem when she hadn't been able to phone her father.

Not that he'd ever maintained contact with her while he was overseas. But he'd always returned to England in October, to celebrate his own birthday in London with his pals. But it was now October, and the chances were that he was home already—home and wondering where she was.

What if her letters to her father and staff had gone astray?

The earlier ones she could imagine him not bothering to answer. But after she'd invited him to her wedding? He must either be furious that she'd found a new future for herself, away from him, or he hadn't received the letter.

She was puzzled by the whole thing, but there was nothing she could do about it. Besides, if he hadn't heard, he would do when she and Rayan returned to England on the holiday she'd told Rayan she wanted. She'd face the music then. But this was today, and she refused to allow anything to spoil her happiness.

She rose to catch the sunrise and stood sipping a strong coffee as the world around her broke into life. It never failed to move her. The sound of the muezzin calling the faithful to prayer, the light intensifying on the adobe walls of the palace, the sound of birds filling the air, and the changing color of the sky—from obsidian darkness pricked with brilliant stars, to sudden light. Apricot at first, but swiftly intensifying first to red then back to a pale orange, then to clear light as the sun emerged over the sea, beaming its rays across from the east direct to her door. She smiled and eased herself into the comfortable chair on the balcony, which had an unobstructed view over the Indian Ocean.

But she wasn't allowed much time alone. Soon the loud tones of Salma—the friend she'd made at the desert camp and who Rayan had brought to keep her company while he was away—broke the silence.

"Lauren! Come, now, you should get ready!"

Lauren smiled at her friend's bossy voice and pushed herself out of the chair. She took the piece of flatbread with halloumi which Salma offered her, and followed her back into the room.

"Here it is!" said Salma and uncovered Lauren's wedding gown, holding it up to admire. "It looks even more beautiful than when you were last fitted." She held it up to Lauren's swelling stomach. "You were right to choose such a loose design. You don't need to advertise to everyone how pregnant you are."

"I think most people know and I'm not embarrassed by it, nor do I wish to hide it."

Salma gave her a sideways look, which Lauren had come to know. Salma disapproved of Lauren's pregnancy before marriage and conveyed it in every way except words. "You English... Anyway, let's do your make-up first."

"Make-up? I don't wear much make-up."

"You're a bride today, Lauren, and not just any bride. You must do your husband proud. He would expect it."

"No," said Lauren firmly. "A little more than usual, maybe, but no kohl, and no bright lipstick or rouge." She turned to the mirror. "I want it to be subtle."

Again the sideways look. This time Salma added a click to the tongue and a sigh. "I don't know what people will think about there being no family on your side. No *Al Khoutha,* no proposal and no family negotiations. It doesn't seem right."

"Rayan can hardly negotiate with my father when we can't track him down. Anyway, it doesn't matter. This is just between Rayan and me. It's *our* marriage and we'll do it our way."

Salma shot her a wide smile. "Of course. That is all that

matters." She shrugged as she twisted the dress so the silk shimmered in the light. "I have never seen a couple more in love than you and our sheikh." She lifted the dress up and held it up against Lauren. "And he will love you even more when he sees you in this."

Lauren's smile faltered over the word love. It wasn't a word that Rayan had ever uttered. She wasn't even sure if Rayan would know love when he saw it. Sometimes she was scared that he *did* know and that he simply didn't love her. But it hadn't put her off marrying him. She knew, quite clearly, that she loved him, and she knew that she'd do everything in her power to make him love her. And she also knew, quite clearly, that Rayan had powerful feelings for her—whatever they were called.

Lauren took the dress from Salma and hung it up.

"We will soon find out." Lauren glanced toward the door where a beautiful, heavily made-up woman had appeared. "Looks like it's time for make-up."

In the end Lauren gave in to Salma's wish for kohl to be applied around the eyes and for more color to be added to her makeup than usual. She had to admit that she looked different. She pulled the hand mirror back and forward, adjusting the angle.

"Well?" asked Salma, with her arms crossed and a big smile revealing perfect white teeth. "Do you approve?"

"Wow! I look really different."

"You look," said Salma triumphantly, "like one of us. A pale one of us obviously, but one of us nevertheless."

"Good. Because that's all I want to be now. Someone who fits into Rayan's world."

"You don't have to look like you fit in, you simply do." Salma walked over to the dress and slipped off its cover, and held it up. "Ready?"

"Absolutely."

. . .

THE WHITE DRESS wasn't traditional Bedouin, but was richly embellished with traditional, fine hand embroidery in cream and gold down the front and back of the dress and the sleeves. She wore one piece of jewelry which Rayan had given her the previous night. It had been his mother's. It was an elaborate necklace of silver studded with coral and pearl. She fingered it as she remembered what he'd said when he'd given it to her. He'd told her he knew his mother would approve of his choice because she'd always valued coral for its meaning as much as for its beauty. He'd told her that when he'd first seen her wearing a coral necklace, he'd make a connection inside which he'd refused to consider at the time. But now he did.

She fingered the necklace. Peace and transformation. That was what his mother had said it represented. She'd said that Rayan would need the first to find the second—embracing a new future. She couldn't argue with that.

She turned to look at Salma and the other women who, apparently, had been essential to helping Lauren prepare for the big day. It had made the morning fun, thought Lauren, listening to the loud chatter and laughter such as had never filled the halls of her old manor. And, for a moment, she wondered if her father was there now, in Norfolk, trying to figure out where she was. Then she saw the makeup artist shoot her a guilty look and slide something which looked like a cellphone into her pocket. She'd left the room, pushed out by one of the other women, before Lauren could say anything.

"Lauren, are you ready?" asked Salma gently. "It's time."

Lauren sucked in an unsteady breath, instantly forgetting what she'd thought she'd seen. It must have been a mistake. Cellphones didn't operate outside of the city. That's what she'd been told, anyway.

She nodded and turned to Salma. "I'm ready."

. . .

RAYAN PACED THE ROOM, unable to contain his agitation. What the hell was he doing? He must be mad!

"Rayan!" growled his brother Adam. "Will you stop your pacing, you're driving me crazy."

But Rayan didn't stop. He hardly heard Adam's words.

Adam stood, hands on hips, staring at Rayan from under a lowered brow, his eyes dark. "Tell him, Zeeshan. He's obviously not going to listen to me."

Rayan felt Zeeshan's hand on his shoulder. "Brother. Stop." Zeeshan's deep, calm voice penetrated Rayan's turbulent thoughts like nothing else could. "Tell me what's troubling you."

Rayan faced him squarely. "I'm getting married. Isn't that enough?"

"No."

"I'm getting married to a woman who I've used as a tool of revenge to get at her father. Is *that* not enough?"

"No. These things we already know."

Suddenly all the fight drained out of Rayan, and he closed his eyes briefly and sighed. "I'm getting married to a woman I'm terrified will walk away from me once she knows the truth. Is *that* enough?"

Zeeshan nodded. "Yes. But there is nothing you can do about it. You must carry on and pray to God that she has found enough in you to love to compensate for what you did before—what all three of us did before. We all agreed. You were simply the one who carried it out."

Adam came over and stood before Rayan. "It'll have to be a miracle to keep them together after Lauren discovers what happened."

Rayan swore under his breath and Zeeshan glared at Adam, who put up his hands in mock surrender. "What? I'm only saying what you two aren't. That such a betrayal isn't the best grounds for a long marriage. That's all I'm saying." He walked away. "I'll give it a month," he said more quietly. Rayan swore again.

"Don't listen to him, Rayan," said Zeeshan. "Adam knows nothing of relationships."

Adam turned to them. "What?" he asked in disbelief. "I adore women and have as many as I can."

"My point exactly." Zeeshan turned back to Rayan. "It's time. Go out there and marry the woman who will be the mother of your child. And, given luck and time, your marriage will flourish."

Rayan couldn't help seeing Adam shoot Zeeshan a skeptical glance, but he ignored it. The die was cast. He would be married that day and the future would take its course. It was out of his hands now.

RAYAN, along with seemingly the rest of the small gathering, stared at Lauren. She didn't look like his Lauren. She appeared taller somehow, more glamorous and entirely at ease in the castle's grand hall. It was only when she glanced at him and gave him that secret warm smile that he was reassured. It didn't stop him from continuing to stare at her. He didn't think he'd ever get enough of her.

She stood beside him, listening more intently than he was, to the imam who was talking about how the Prophet honored his wives and how men should honor their wives, and how women should treat their husbands and honor them. For Rayan, the word 'honor' was used too frequently for comfort, considering the deceit underlying this whole wedding. And once Lauren discovered exactly how dishonorable he'd been, he knew she wouldn't stand for it. He just prayed he'd be given enough time to convince her to stay with him.

Then the imam turned to Rayan, and he was forced to take his eyes off Lauren. The imam instructed Rayan to heed the speech he'd just given and then Zeeshan stepped forward, standing in for Lauren's father. As if in a dream, the ceremony continued with each person fulfilling their part until the legal documents were completed and signed. The marriage contract, thought Rayan, fingering it lightly before setting it onto the table—*his* marriage contract.

With a nudge from Zeeshan, he slipped the rings from Lauren's right hand to her left index finger. Impulsively, he kissed her fingers and then let her hand drop suddenly at the surprised laughter which ensued. The laughter continued as the rituals drew to a close and the festivities began.

The musicians began to play and Rayan knew what was demanded of him. How could he forget? He'd been forced to practice with Lauren twice a day over the past week.

The first dance went better than expected. Even so, Rayan was pleased to take a seat beside his beautiful new bride. He watched her while she watched the dancing. She turned to him suddenly, and a smile bloomed.

"You're not watching what's going on, are you?"

"Of course I am. I'm watching the only person worth watching in the room—you."

She lifted his hand, which enveloped hers in a possessive grip, and kissed each of his knuckles in turn. "A kiss," she said turning to the next knuckle, "for each time you kiss me in a place on my body which I shall request later, when we're alone."

"Your request is my command. I am your slave, my lady." He inclined his head.

She kissed another knuckle. "I'm glad to hear it."

There was a call, and she turned with a blush back to Rayan. "They're all looking at us. It's time to cut the cake."

Rayan did as he was told, moved where he was required, and joined the applause when, after the cake-cutting, Lauren tossed her bouquet into the air, which somehow landed in Adam's hands. He dropped it immediately, and it was plucked from the floor by Salma. Then he and Lauren led their guests into a reception room for the wedding feast. It was all a blur except for Lauren, who shone like a beacon of hope, her eyes alight with laughter and love, giving him a hope for the future that he hardly dared have before. Maybe, just maybe, Zeeshan was correct. Everything *would* all be all right.

MUCH LATER, Lauren watched from the castle balcony along with her two brothers-in-law as guns were fired across the harbor to celebrate their wedding. She suddenly felt a little tired.

"I'm going to sit this one out, Rayan," she shouted in his ear, trying to be heard above the noise of the festivities and guns.

He turned and kissed her, caressing her cheeks and searching her face. "Are you well? Is it the baby?"

She laughed and shook her head. "It's only the baby in so far as I'm tired. It's been a long day. I want to put my feet up for ten minutes."

"I'll come with you."

"No. You stay here with your brothers. I'll be fine. There's nothing you can do, anyway."

She took one last look at the three men lined up along the edge of the balcony, looking out at the dark harbor and the fireworks which lit up the skies. She could hardly believe her luck. That she should have found someone like Rayan, and that he wanted her as his wife, still seemed incredible to her. She thought she'd never been so happy in her life before.

Smiling to herself, she stepped into the small sitting room which had been Rayan's mother's and which she used as her own private domain. She was surprised to see Salma come in through the main door.

"Is everything okay, Salma? I thought you'd be dancing!"

"I was. But, my friend"—she gripped Lauren's hands and grinned—"it looks like my wish has been answered and someone from your family has turned up after all."

Lauren's mouth fell open, and she stared, speechless, at Salma.

Salma laughed. "Have you nothing to say about this?"

Lauren spluttered. Trouble was, she had too much to say. "Is it my father?"

Salma's smile fell. "No, I'm sorry, it isn't. It's a woman who says she's a relative of yours."

Lauren's brow furrowed. "A woman relative?" She had an ancient aunt, but she didn't think she'd jump on a jet and come to the Middle East to track down her errant niece. "Who is it?"

Salma shrugged. "I'll let her in and you can see who it is for yourself." She squeezed her hands. "I'm so happy for you."

Lauren watched Salma leave the room. The door was immediately opened, and a woman stepped inside—a woman Lauren knew well. But she was no relative.

"Angela! What on earth are you doing here?" Lauren gave the woman a hug, a hug that was barely reciprocated. It never had been. "How lovely that you could be here for my wedding. A little late, maybe, but lovely all the same."

"I'm not here for your wedding, Lauren. I'm here as your father's attorney."

"Oh." Lauren was mystified. "So he received my letters?"

"Letters?" It was Angela's turn to look mystified. "What

letters?"

"I sent him letters. Every week I wrote to him, asking him to come."

"He didn't get them. But I'm sure you'll see why he didn't get them when I disclose the reason for my visit."

Lauren tilted her head to one side, desperately trying to understand what was going on. She opened her mouth to speak, but shook her head instead.

Angela cleared her throat. "I can see you were the innocent party in all of this, which makes it all the worse. Your father didn't receive any communications from you, or anyone else you are… connected to. He returned to England a week ago and was surprised to find you not in residence."

Lauren felt a flicker of anger at hearing that her father hadn't even been aware of her absence until a week ago.

"If he'd bothered to contact anyone on the estate prior to that, he'd have discovered it sooner. Where was he? In the Caribbean? Or had he moved to a more remote island, somewhere where the relatives of his current mistress couldn't track him down?"

Angela had the grace to look discomfited. Lauren reckoned she'd got it right first time. "He was… busy. I'm not at liberty to elaborate."

"Busy. Right." Lauren mulled over what her father could be so busy with that could have prevented him from coming to her wedding. There was only reason which could excuse his absence. "Is he well?"

"Perfectly."

"He couldn't even be bothered to come here, could he, not even for my wedding?"

Before Angela could answer, there was a noise at the door and they both turned to see Rayan, silhouetted against the sky, in which fireworks continued to spray gloriously across the indigo sky.

"Lauren! What's going on?" In a couple of strides, he was beside her. He put his arm around her, and she was so glad to lean into his strength. She tried, unsuccessfully, to blink back the tears. Incensed, Rayan turned to Angela. "Who the hell are you and how dare you invade our privacy and upset my wife on our wedding day?"

"Ah, so you must be the sheikh we've heard so much about."

"I am Sheikh Rayan ibn Mohammed Aziz. And who, may I ask, are you? And what are you doing here?"

"I am Angela Wareing and I'm Charles le Harivel's attorney. And I'm here to inform your *wife,* that she's been duped by you. That this"—Angela waved her hand in a wide flourish — "is all part of a grand deception."

Lauren suddenly felt faint, and if it hadn't been for Rayan's arm around her, she would have fallen. She tried to move but found his grip had tightened and it was too tight. She could feel the imprint of his fingers pressing into her flesh. She tried to wriggle out of it, but his grip held firm.

She swallowed a wave of nausea and forced herself to repeat Angela's words to herself—words which had seemed so bizarre at first that she hadn't absorbed them. But, after the second repetition, she realized that her body's weakness signaled an understanding faster than her mind.

"Could you repeat that?" she asked Angela quietly.

"No!" shouted Rayan. He pointed to the door. "Go, go now. You're not wanted here." He shouted for the guards outside, and Lauren could hear them come running. But they weren't there yet.

"Please, tell me," Lauren asked Angela. "What do you mean by 'grand deception?'"

"Isn't it obvious?" said Angela, just as a guard descended on her and took her roughly by the arm. "All this." She glared at Rayan. "He doesn't want you to know. He came to England for one purpose only—to seduce you. He wanted to seduce you, make you pregnant and then discard you."

"No." Lauren refused to look at Rayan, whose grip was still firm on his arm. "No. Why would he?"

"Because of what your father did to his sister." It seemed Angela no longer cared about protecting her client's reputation. "He seduced her, she became pregnant and then he left her, and she killed herself."

"Nooo..." The word slipped from her mouth like a groan, and she looked up at Rayan, dreading what she might see in his face. "No, please Rayan, tell me she's wrong. Tell me that that didn't happen."

He stared hard at her, opened his mouth to speak, but closed it again before uttering a sound.

"You see, he can't, because it's the truth," said Angela. "You do remember Madaniya, don't you?"

"Yes, I remember her. She came to the estate once with Dad." She looked up at Rayan, unable to understand. Surely she'd missed a vital piece of information? "Rayan? What's going on. Do you really have a sister called Madaniya?"

"I *had* a sister called Madaniya. She was everything to me. And she died, because of your father."

Ice slithered down her veins, ridding it of the nausea but making everything else so much worse. It was like a fog had lifted, and the pieces to the puzzle formed a hideously clear pattern. And she knew it had been one that had been there all along. She just hadn't wanted to see the truth.

"And you came to England to work on my family's estate as a stable-hand—something I could never understand—for one purpose only—to get your own back on my father? Is this for real?"

He gave one short nod. It was all she needed. The world

suddenly swam around her and she staggered. He tried to hold her, but she pulled herself away.

"You see!" shouted Angela from the doorway through which she was being pulled by the guards. "He only wanted you to get back at your father. And that is why I'm here. To call this marriage the sham that it is."

"Get her out of here!" shouted Rayan to the guards.

Lauren didn't watch Angela leave, just knew she'd gone by the silence which ensued. She sat down and put her head in her hands, and tried to gulp down air to calm herself. It didn't work.

Then she felt his touch on her shoulder. "Lauren," said Rayan, his voice close, too close.

She leaped up. "Don't touch me!" Suddenly, from feeling weak, she felt anger coursing through her veins, reaching out to every part of her, controlling her, taking over her thoughts and feelings. There was nothing else but this blind, white anger charging her speech. "Don't you dare touch me!"

Clearly shocked, Rayan almost stumbled back under the onslaught of her words.

There were no tears as she approached him and, when it emerged, her voice was icy calm. "You tricked me. You seduced me, so easily, and you got me pregnant because you said you had no condoms. No condoms, huh? And I was such a needy fool that I fell for it all. Even your lack of charm charmed me. I bet you were laughing with your brothers to find your revenge so easily accomplished, weren't you?"

"No, my darling, no—"

"Don't 'my darling' me. We are *nothing* to each other now. *Nothing*. God knows why you wanted to go through a wedding ceremony. Was that simply going one better than my father? Get me married before dumping me."

"No—"

"Don't talk to me! I want you to *listen* to me. I want you to know that you might have thought you were doing something bad to me. But you know what? I got exactly what I wanted from you. I got a child. I longed for a child for years, and you gave me one. *Thank you*. And if I don't have to have *you*, then so much the better!"

She stared at him with her new steely gaze while she wrenched off the ring, which he'd only just pushed onto her finger and then threw it at him.

"Keep it. You can use it for the next woman you seduce."

She just managed to leave the room for her bedroom before she broke down in tears.

# CHAPTER 10

Lauren had given instructions not to be disturbed, and she wasn't. She didn't know how long she sat on the edge of the bed staring out to sea. She was as still as her thoughts and emotions were turbulent—darting from one thing to another, but always leading back to the same two things.

She'd been used by both her father and her lover, and she wasn't the same woman she'd been in Norfolk.

Whether she liked it or not, Rayan had opened her eyes, her heart and her mind to the world. She was a stronger woman than she was before. And she refused to be anybody's fool, anybody's puppet, any longer.

It was only when she began shivering that she looked at the clock with a start. It was late. Or rather, it was the early hours of the next day. It would be light soon.

Still wearing her wedding dress, she climbed under the covers and closed her eyes. She was prepared to wait, unsleeping until dawn, but her exhaustion proved inescapable because the next thing she knew, bright sunshine was flooding the room.

Before she'd gone to bed she'd thought of many things, but her future had eluded her. But now, in the vibrant light of morning, she knew what she was going to do with a certainty which was unshakeable. She was going to stay here. It was in *this* country where she had found herself, her love, and her baby. And she wanted to stay here. There was nothing but defeat in returning to Norfolk, where she'd resume her old role except without the respect she used to have. And she refused to take that role—of meek, put-upon woman, any longer.

She rose, noting for the first time that she was still dressed in her wedding dress. She stripped it off immediately, looked at it for a moment as she remembered the happiness and hopes she'd felt when she'd put it on. She placed it to one side. She just wished she could place everything else to one side as easily.

Once showered and dressed, she did what she should have done months earlier. She made her way through the castle's main reception rooms into the warren of small rooms which comprised the administration offices. She met no one on the way, nor anyone inside the suite of rooms. To celebrate the wedding, a day's holiday had been given to everyone, and she intended to take full advantage of it.

She closed the door behind her and looked around. Why hadn't she been here before? It was true that Rayan had made excuses about communications, but it was also true that she hadn't pushed it. Maybe her need to believe him was stronger than her doubts. She shook her head in despair. She hated that she'd been so weak.

It didn't take long before she found what she'd been looking for—a telephone connected to a landline, which had been so conspicuously absent from the main castle. Now she knew why there were connections in the wall, but no phones.

The phone was hidden behind some filing baskets. She lifted it from the cradle and put it to her ear. It emitted a loud and clear dial tone—a sound which proved she'd been taken for a fool.

She knew the number off by heart. It rang twice before it was picked up. He must have been expecting it.

"Dad," she said softly, moved by the familiar gruff tones of her father.

"Lauren, darling!" Her father's clear voice of authority cut through the miles between them and hit her hard, where it hurt most, in the heart.

She wound the cord around her finger, blinking with the sudden rush of emotion. "Daddy," she said, reverting to her child-like name for him. "I've missed you." She swept away a tear.

"And I've missed you, too. If only I'd known what was going on, I'd have dropped everything and come for you."

Despite her sadness, instinctively Lauren knew he was lying. Her father's love for her had always been something to show off in front of others. Everyone had always commented on how she was the apple of his eye—everyone who wasn't close to him, that is. But she knew otherwise. The pretense had always ended when the audience had left. Still, he was the only father she had, and she loved him, no matter what he thought of her.

"How did you know, Dad? How did you find out about Rayan… and me? Was it the letter I left for you?"

"I *never* received a letter from you, darling. I daresay *he* made sure I didn't!"

Lauren was about to defend Rayan before remembering that she hadn't been the last one to leave the library, where she'd left the letter for her father. Rayan had. Her mouth dried. "Anyway." She cleared her throat. "I've seen Angela."

"Good. She told you the whole thing? How that, that

*foreigner* used you cruelly to get back at me? She told you that?"

She couldn't admit to that yet—maybe to herself, but not to her father. "She told me about you and Madaniya—Rayan's half-sister. That she was pregnant."

Her father was silent for a few moments. "I swear I didn't know until after..."

"After she died," said Lauren dully. The similarities between her and Madaniya were inescapable—both seduced by charismatic men before their affairs came to an inevitable conclusion. But she was determined she wouldn't suffer the same fate. "Angela told me about Rayan's reaction to her affair with you. But, I need to know, Dad. Did you know she died?"

"No, not straight away. A mutual friend told me."

She closed her eyes tightly, trying to rid herself of the image of Madaniya deserted and alone and her father continuing to party thousands of miles away.

"So, tell me, how did you know about Rayan?" She was hoping beyond hope that there was a flaw somewhere which would show Rayan in a better light.

"Despite what you'd told them, our staff suspected you'd gone off with him, and showed me the HR file when I arrived here a week ago. It contained a photograph, and I recognized him from one Madaniya had once shown me. It only took a few phone calls to put two and two together."

"Can we take it more slowly, Dad? How could you put two and two together? What makes you so sure this was an act of revenge? I mean, it's a pretty antiquated concept, isn't it?"

"It's obvious, isn't it? Why else do you think he'd have come to England to work on the estate? Why else would he have tried to seduce you? Come on, think! It's hardly happened before, has it?"

"No," she whispered into the phone. "It hasn't." A year ago she would have accepted what her father said with all its implications—she wasn't a suitable object for seduction, she wasn't worthy of love. But things had changed during the past few months; *she'd* been changed by loving the very man who'd tried to ruin her life. She grunted at the irony. He'd tried to harm her but had, in the end, given her the life she'd craved for years. Or a version of it.

"Come home, darling," her father said, in his most wheedling voice. "Everything is the same here and we can sort out your little problem."

Lauren wondered if she'd heard correctly. "My little problem?"

"I heard about your pregnancy. If it's too late to abort, we can have it adopted out."

She looked at the phone in disgust before putting it back against her ear. "He's not an 'it'."

"Whatever. Come home and we can continue as we have been. You'll be safe here."

"Safe," she repeated faintly. Safe and childless while her father left her to run the family business once more. She cleared her throat and stood up. "I'll let you know what I decide. Goodbye, Dad. I'll be in touch."

She replaced the phone and walked to the nearest window, throwing it open and gulping down the morning air. Despite what her father had told her, she felt panicked at the thought of returning to the home which had, now she realized, felt more like a prison. And, if she'd had any lingering doubts before, she knew, in that moment, what she most definitely *would not* do. She wasn't that child anymore—she was a strong woman who'd take control of her life.

She closed the window firmly and walked back to the main castle, not to her bedroom, but to where she guessed Rayan and his brothers would be.

. . .

RAYAN JUMPED up when the door burst open and Lauren entered the library, looking like a force to be reckoned with. She wasn't wearing a scarf and her blonde hair flew behind her as she entered the room.

"Lauren!"

He could hear his two brothers move behind him. They were all accustomed to people rising to meet them, used to obedience and barking orders, used to everyone—especially women—being subservient to them. And yet here they were —three grown men—speechless in front of the slight woman with a fire in her eyes.

"Yes," she said, closing the door and turning to face them, her usually smiling face firmly in command. "Were you expecting someone else?"

"No, I—"

"Good, because I wanted to see you."

There were mutterings from Adam and Zeeshan, and Zeeshan cleared his throat. "I think it best we leave, I—"

"And I think it best you stay," said Lauren, in her clear English voice. "It involves you all. Please, take a seat, this shouldn't take long."

To Rayan's surprise, both Zeeshan and Adam sat down. Even more to his surprise, he found himself doing the same thing. All three men looked up at Lauren, who strode to the middle of the room where she could best be seen. She didn't take a seat, she didn't lean against any chair or wall. It didn't appear that this fearsome woman before him—his wife, he reminded himself—needed any support whatsoever.

"I've been talking with my father on the telephone. Yes, Rayan, you might well look like that. A telephone which you said was out of order. Another stupid lie which I swallowed because I trusted you."

Rayan didn't think he'd ever felt so low. "You *can* trust me."

"Really?" Sarcasm dripped from the word. She took a step towards him. As they were all seated, she loomed over them, all five foot two of her. "You *really* think I can trust you. That's very interesting, and very incorrect. You appear to have no knowledge of the meaning of the word 'trust'."

"What Rayan is trying to say," said Zeeshan, "is that he's changed."

She turned an icy stare on Zeeshan, who blinked in surprise. "Thank you, Your Majesty, for that interjection. But I hardly think I'm going to believe you either."

"And why not?"

"Because you—all of you—are as culpable as each other. You *all* wanted to punish my father for what he did, and you all chose me—an innocent party—as a tool for that punishment."

Adam jumped up. "This is ridiculous."

"Sit down," bellowed Lauren, in a tone and strength of voice which Rayan hadn't known existed within that slight body.

Muttering, Adam did as he was told.

"That's better. I want all three of you here because I want you all to be clear about what I'm going to do."

She paused, but each of the three men had obviously decided that silence was their best option.

"No doubt you imagine that, with my trust in Rayan destroyed, knowing that he has never loved me—of course he's never said as much, but I'd hoped…" Her voice wobbled a little on the last word and Rayan jumped up, desperate to bridge the gap between them and to put his arms around her and hold her until the iciness had melted, revealing the real Lauren once more. But he received another glacial stare, and he took his seat once more. "No doubt you imagine that with the marriage obviously a sham that I'd run away, retreat to England to lick my wounds."

She paused, and there was nothing but an expectant silence as all three men held their breath in anticipation of her reply. Goodness knows they'd spent long enough debating it over the night, with all three coming up with different scenarios which they each thought was best, but which none of them agreed on. There was nothing they could do. It was down to her, and they all knew it.

"But I'm not. I'm going to stay, here in the castle. I am your wife, Rayan. I'm carrying your child and I'm happy here. Or I *was* happy here, but I will be again. This is *my* home now, and the home of my child."

"*Our* child," he couldn't help saying. She shot him a filthy look.

She obviously decided to pretend he hadn't said anything. Instead, she put her hands on her hips and glared at each of them in turn.

"I want it known that I'm not someone you can sweep under the carpet, someone you can hide away, someone you can try to hurt and then conveniently set aside. I want you to know that I'm here to stay and that you had better all get used to the idea. Each of you. Because you are all guilty in my eyes. As guilty as my father is. You're all as bad as him. Haven't any of you ever asked yourselves what you sister would make of all of this? Do you really think she'd be proud of you? Or isn't there just a little voice inside of each of you wondering if she's condemning you, hating you, for repeating the same crimes as my father? Of inflicting the same casual, but deadly, pain on a woman who didn't deserve it?" She nodded, as if aware that that was exactly what they were all thinking. Her gaze settled on Rayan. "And it's not me, it's *you*, who will have to live knowing that you're no better than him. And not just *no* better, but a whole lot worse."

Rayan jumped up. "Okay, Lauren, we've heard what you have to say. Now it's only fair that you listen to me."

"Fair? Since when have you played fair?"

"Over to you, Rayan," said Adam, jumping up and making immediately for the door.

Zeeshan also rose but walked over to Lauren, who had to lift her gaze. "I'm more sorry than I can express, Lauren. All I can say in our defense is that our world, our culture, and"—he shot a look at Rayan—"our personal experiences with our family has created three people with a very different world-view to your own. It doesn't excuse us maybe, but hopefully, at some point, you'll understand us. In the meantime, I'll leave you two alone. Because, whatever you may think, you need to talk to Rayan alone."

Rayan could see that Zeeshan's reasoned words had cut through Lauren's bravado, and the look she gave Rayan gave him hope. There was hurt behind the cool facade and hurt meant she still had feelings for him—maybe even loved him. He could work with love. He waited until they were alone.

"I'm sorry, Lauren. I'm *so* sorry."

"You're sorry that I found out?"

"No, of course not. I knew you would find out eventually."

"So you don't deny any of it."

It was only then he realized that there was a part of her which hoped that he'd refute all charges against him.

"No. It's true, I did set out to avenge my sister's death."

"And I was collateral damage. Caught in the cross-fire."

"Yes. And I'm sorry you were. I'd never expected that I would feel…" He trailed off, unable to complete the sentence, unable to analyze his feelings.

"Feel what? Please tell me, I'm dying to hear."

"I... I..." Words failed him, as they usually did when he had to consider his emotions. He was out of his depth.

She swallowed and shifted her weight from one foot to another as she crossed her arms. "Oh, please stop. It's painful to watch."

He could only take so much. "No, Lauren, you stop. Hear me out. All I know is that you've changed me. I might have started out with a plan for revenge, but I most certainly didn't end up succeeding. "

Uncertainty flickered over her face. "I changed you, and how exactly did I do that?"

"Through your love for me. You loved me then and you love me now." He stepped towards her and the veil of anger lifted fully from her eyes, revealing the tender woman beneath. She gulped. "And I've been changed forever by it. I'm not the same man I was all those months ago when I was hired to look after your horses. And that's down to you."

"You think I should be proud of the change I've made in you?" Her voice was less strident now.

He shrugged. "It's up to you how you feel about it. I'm simply stating my case. Look, I understand you're angry with me—"

"You know what, Rayan?" Her voice had lowered another tone. "I'm actually more angry with myself than with you, or my father. Angry at my weakness at being duped by you both. You're both the same. Cut from the same cloth. Both amoral. At least he doesn't pretend to be anything different. But you? You think you're some defender of truth, some high and mighty person who can make judgements and dish out punishments. But no one should be able to do that to another person. Remember that old Bible verse? 'If anyone of you is without sin, let him be the first to throw a stone.' I don't think you're one of those, are you?"

Her mouth twisted into a heart-breaking grimace, and

she turned to walk away. He stepped forward between her and the door, desperate to stop her.

"Lauren, please. Tell me what I can do to make you see how sorry I am for what I've done."

She turned around, and it was almost worse seeing her pitying expression. "I know how sorry you are, Rayan. That's easy to see. What I don't know is whether I can trust you."

"You can. You *can* trust me."

"You really think that's all you have to do? Just say the words and trust is re-established? Rayan, it doesn't work like that."

He was so close to her now that he could have easily overpowered her, have taken her in his arms and done all the things he knew she loved to make her weaken. But he forced himself to stay still. That might work for an hour, or even a night, but it wouldn't work long term, and long term was all he wanted with her now.

"Then tell me how it does work," he said between gritted teeth.

"I don't know how this works," she said wearily, putting her hand on the door. "But, if neither of us are leaving the castle, then I guess we're going to find out one way or another."

She opened the door and stepped into the hallway.

"I'll prove to you, Lauren, if it's the last thing I do, that you can trust me and that we have a future together." She hesitated and looked down, but didn't turn to face him.

"Well, God knows how you're going to do that, because I don't have a clue."

He watched her walk across the hall and up the stairs to her suite of rooms. He closed the door wearily and sat down, his head in his hands.

He sure hoped God knew, and that he told him, because he hadn't a clue either.

# CHAPTER 11

"*Sabah jamil*!" Salma entered Lauren's room the next morning and opened the curtains wide as if nothing had happened. "It looks like the weather is closing in a little." She squinted into the sky. "I think there might be a storm coming." She turned to Lauren and looked at her acutely. "Are you well? We were all told to make ourselves scarce." She gave Lauren a conspiratorial grin. "We imagined our sheikh wanted you and the castle to yourselves."

Lauren glanced at the other half of the bed, which remained undisturbed. It was obvious Rayan hadn't slept in it. Salma followed her glance and frowned. Then she shrugged and went to the wardrobe and flung it open. She swept her gaze across the clothes, and Lauren realized her friend wasn't looking at the clothes but was quietly trying to make sense of a deserted castle and a deserted bed. She knew she was right when Salma closed the doors without extracting any clothes and turned to Lauren.

"What's the matter? Something's wrong, isn't it?"

Lauren tried to smile but failed, and swung her legs out of

bed and pushed her hands through her hair. She looked up at Salma and nodded. "Yes, something is very wrong."

Salma muttered oaths which Lauren had only heard drifting up from the fishermen in the harbor below the castle. "I knew it. What's happened?"

Lauren shrugged, wondering how to sum up all that had happened. "I've been tricked." She blinked lightly, desperately trying to repress the swell of emotion which threatened to destroy her control.

Salma's eyes narrowed. "Tricked? Into marriage? But you wished to get married, did you not?"

Lauren nodded. "I did."

"Tricked into having sex with our sheikh? You never appeared to be a woman who was being taken advantage of."

"I wasn't."

"Then how were you tricked?"

"I thought"—she swallowed—"I thought he had feelings for me."

"Of course he does. Everyone can see that. Everyone is talking about that. It cannot only be you who doesn't know!"

"There was only one reason he wanted me and that was to avenge his sister's death. You see, she died because of my father."

Understanding dawned on Salma's face. "Ah, I'm beginning to understand. Of course we heard about what happened to Sheikha Madaniya, but we didn't know it was connected with you." She rubbed her lips with her fist thoughtfully. "And so our sheikh sought you out with this in mind." She nodded, not waiting for an answer before continuing. "You do not understand, Lauren. Our people—our culture, our ways—are different to yours."

"I know there are differences, but you are right, I *don't* understand. I don't understand how people can destroy someone who is entirely innocent to get back at someone else. It's barbaric."

Salma's frown deepened. "No, it's not barbaric. It's just different."

"We're never going to agree on this, Salma. Our worlds are poles apart. What Rayan did is unforgivable."

"No, my friend, no. Sheikh Rayan is a fine man. He is a good man and deeply loyal, otherwise he would not have done such a thing. He has married you, which shows that you are now his and he will protect you with his life."

"I don't want to belong to someone. I don't want someone to protect me with his life. I want someone to love me and, Salma, I truly don't believe he can love anyone. There are things which happened in his past which I only know a little of, which made him a man incapable of love."

"I know what his father did to him. Everyone knows of that. It shows our sheikh's strength that he has become the man he is despite that."

"But he is so strong." She pressed her hand against one of the castle's thick walls, which had withstood centuries of tribal warfare and marauding foreign armies. "He's like this castle—so strong that nothing, and no one can get through. He can't feel, let alone show love."

"But he takes you to his bed all the time. That is a show of love."

Lauren had a sudden memory of their explosive lovemaking. Was that love? Or was it lust? Did Salma have a point?

"I don't know. Maybe he can be like that with anyone. I have so little experience, I just don't know. But it was what he set out to do—take me for a mistress to avenge my father—and he has never spoken a word of love."

For a moment, a look of uncertainty filled Salma's expressive face. But it quickly vanished.

"There is more to marriage than love. Many of us have

arranged marriages and love comes later, but it usually comes. Don't give up on him."

Lauren shook her head, unable to answer Salma's plea. Suddenly, the door banged close.

"Thank you for the character reference, Salma. But you may leave now."

They both turned to the door where Rayan stood. Lauren didn't know how long he'd stood there listening to their conversation. And it seemed Salma wasn't going to hang around to find out. She made a swift exit, closing the door firmly behind her.

Lauren tied her gown around her defensively. "How long have you been there?"

"Long enough."

"For what?"

Rayan glanced around the room, checked the contents of the wardrobe, and then closed the door and stood looking at Lauren. "To hear that you don't think I can love."

"Well, can you?"

He shrugged. "I agree with Salma. People marry and then"—he waved his hand dismissively—"their feelings grow. It's as simple as that."

"Simple, eh?" She shot him a wistful smile. She only wished it were that simple.

"It could be, if you let it be."

Could it really be that easy? For a moment, as she looked into Rayan's eyes, she could almost believe it. But then the sunlight flickered and was then extinguished, casting his face into shadow. Even the light was playing tricks on her, deceiving her.

She glanced out the window and saw the storm clouds Salma had predicted creeping over the sky, and casting the entire land, not just Rayan, into shadow. It was the first time since she'd arrived that the sun hadn't shone brightly. It felt as if the entire world was trying to tell her something. And she knew what it was. The days of innocence and trust were over.

"Oh, Rayan. Nothing's simple." She pressed her palm to her forehead and eyes, trying to relieve the mounting pressure. It didn't work. "How can I simply go on, trusting that you'll grow to love me when you've destroyed the trust I had not only in you, but in my own judgement? I hardly know what's true about anything anymore."

A wave of nausea swept over her, and the room spun. She staggered, and he reached out and steadied her.

"Are you all right, *habibti*? Are you ill?"

Lauren pressed her eyes tight shut, and he held her close. Despite all her rational thoughts, she felt safe here in his arms. That couldn't be wrong, could it? Every part of her melted into him like she was coming home. She sucked in a deep breath to better breathe in his scent. Despite herself, she felt her body ignite with desire.

She took another breath, which became ragged in her throat as her heartbeat quickened. She looked up to find him looking down at her, their mouths nearly touching. He cupped her face with his hands, searched her face for any sign of refusal and, finding none, pressed his lips to hers and gave her the kind of kiss she needed—deep, passionate and all-consuming. A kiss to wipe away distressing thoughts, conflicting beliefs, and give her one pure thing they both could agree on. Their need for one another's bodies and the obliteration of rational thought.

She pressed herself against him and his hands slipped under the robe and caressed her naked skin, moving lower to her bottom. He pulled her against him, and she could feel how hard he was for her.

She gasped and let her head fall back as his lips lowered onto her neck. Without a word, he carried her across to the bed. There he laid her gently onto the white sheet and opened her robe, revealing her nakedness. It should have felt wrong—she should have covered her nakedness—but instead she reached out for his hand and kissed it. She looked up at him and saw the dark flare of lust in his eyes, along with indecision. She took his hand and, all the while watching him, sucked on his fingers, remembering how clever they were when they explored her body.

The indecision lifted and with a groan he pulled his hand away. He gave her rounded belly a brief caress before stepping away and pulling off his clothes.

With one swift movement, he'd lifted her hips and thrust deep inside of her. There was no friction, despite the suddenness of the lovemaking. It seemed she was always ready for him, always wet for him to fill her, to make her complete.

Her eyelids fluttered as he remained at her center, and she used her internal muscles to grip him and play with him as she shifted slightly to give herself more of the sensations which flooded her body. She shivered and gasped as a small orgasm rocked her. Then she opened her eyes to find him staring at her. And then he began.

It started slowly, with a withdrawal which slid out of her with excruciating slowness that made her aware of every frisson of sensation. Then he thrust into her deeply again, with more force this time, shunting her slightly back onto the bed. His gaze slid to her stomach, as if remembering the need to be gentle. She wasn't in the mood for gentle. She wanted him to make her forget her doubts and fears and to live in that moment with him.

She gripped his bottom, sinking her fingers into his muscles, pulling her into him. The need she tried to convey in her fingers must have shown in her eyes because, although nothing was said, he no longer held back.

He thrust into her again, but this time didn't stop. Faster and faster he thrust, ratcheting up her pleasure with each thrust, until she gripped the bedclothes, trying to prolong the pleasure. But she couldn't and she cried out his name. Only then did he come inside of her with quick thrusts, closing his eyes—whether in pain or pleasure, she couldn't have said.

And she knew then, as he withdrew and lay down beside her, pulling her into his arms, that wherever she lived, whatever she did, she would always be his woman. There would never be any other man for her.

She couldn't have said how long they lay like that, their breathing slowly returning to normal, his body providing warmth to her as a chill wind crept in through the open window and darkness continued to cover the sun. Then she heard it.

A splattering sound, as if someone had thrown something wet at the castle walls. Except it kept on coming. At first she wondered what the sound was. Then she smelled the damp dust and realized it was rain. There was a clap of thunder and the rain began in earnest, pelting the dry earth and walls of the castle with torrential, bullet-like drops.

She twisted around and stood up, pulled on her robe, and walked across to the window. She opened it wide, and the rain blasted her, instantly soaking her, forming puddles on the stone floor, which trickled over the uneven floor, soaking into the rugs. It was chill, but she welcomed something that would break the spell which Rayan's body had put her under. She needed to listen to her head, not her heart or her body. She stepped outside under the full force of the rain, just as a bolt of lightning rent the steely gray sky.

"You look like a goddess," called Rayan, raising his voice over the thunder of the rain. "And I feel like a mortal man, unworthy of you."

With the water now running off her in thick, ropey

rivulets, outlining her swollen breasts and stomach, she turned to him, hardly able to see through the veil of rain. The brightness of the morning had now completely disappeared into a terrible, savage darkness which felt right. It seemed to Lauren that, ever since they'd first met, they'd been moving toward such a moment as this. She felt as if she were on the summit of a mountain, seeing clearly for the first time, despite the rain that washed over her eyes and cheeks, making Rayan out of focus and blurry.

"I'm sorry, Lauren," Rayan called out, hardly heard above the roar of the rain and the increasing wind. "I'm so sorry."

She suddenly realized that what she'd taken for rain was tears—hers and his. Two strides separated them, but neither moved. Their lovemaking had solved nothing, hadn't brought them any closer. It had only been a thing of temporary comfort. She shivered, and he reached out his hand to hers. She shook her head, rejecting his hand, and stepped out of the rain.

"And I am, too, Rayan. More than I can say."

"Tell me what I can do to make things right."

"I don't know what can be done. How can you set something right which is based on so much wrong?"

"There must be something. Tell me. Whatever it is, I'll do it."

"There's only one thing I've ever wanted, and that's to love and to be loved. I have one, but I don't have the other," she said softly. "And I don't know if you can love me after what you've been through."

"I'll try. I swear I'll try."

She shook her head. "That's not enough. I don't want always to be wondering if I'm enough for you. I don't deserve that, Rayan. Not from you, not from anyone." She pressed her palm to her stomach. "I aim to be a better example to my child, than my parents were to me. I only want the best for my child, and for me."

"Of course." He nodded. "And I will give that to you. I will help you as much as I can. Anything you want, you can have, whatever the price."

"You know what I want, and it doesn't have a price."

Neither said anything for what seemed like an age. It was long enough for a clap of thunder to rise to a crescendo, causing ornaments to rattle, before fading away into the distance, followed by the unearthly light of a fork of lightning which made Rayan look like a creature from another planet—naked, his sex hard and ready for her, his eyes burning like coals.

Despite her need for him, she knew what she had to do. She walked to where he'd left his clothes and tossed them to him.

"Please get dressed and leave," she said, in a gravely voice which threatened to betray her emotions. She balled her hands into fists to stop herself from reaching out to him. Because her words were the opposite of what she wanted to say to him. But she needed to be strong now, otherwise she would always regret it.

"You want me to go?"

"Yes. I can't be with someone I can't trust, someone who is so filled with anger that he takes every opportunity to vent it. Because you can't tell me you didn't jump at the chance to avenge your sister."

She gave him the opportunity to deny her accusation, but he was silent. He might be many things, but he wasn't a liar.

"I thought not. It was an outlet for the anger which is locked inside of you, controlling everything else. And, until you can show me you've changed, that you're not a man consumed by his anger, I don't want you in my life, or our baby's life."

She walked to the door and opened it. He picked up the clothes which he'd strewn across the floor earlier and pulled on his trousers. He walked over to her by the door and stopped so close that she could smell the delicious scent of his body—something which always made not just her mouth moisten. But she managed to hold his fiery gaze calmly.

"I will not give up on you, Lauren. You are my life now. If I need to make changes, I will. I will prove to you I'm worthy of your love." His gaze raked her face as if soaking up every element of her, engraving it into his memory.

The temporary feeling of calm was beginning to shatter, and she turned away, not wanting him to see the tears which were collecting in her eyes. She heard a movement, and she wondered if he would come to her and hold her, and she didn't know what she would do if he did.

She nearly weakened, feeling the urge to turn back to him and allow herself to be comforted. But she waited a fraction too long and when she looked for him, he'd gone. And she knew, then, that she couldn't trust herself while he was near, that she had her own healing to do.

Rayan didn't know where he was going but he kept on walking, shrugging on his shirt as he walked, in bare feet, out of the castle and into the rain which now fell with a sweeping drizzle as the storm passed over. But it didn't feel as if it had passed over for him. It stayed inside him, tormenting him for what he'd done, for the man he'd allowed his past to make him. And for what, because of that, he was about to lose—everything.

He continued walking until he'd left the castle behind him and had reached the sea, which was churning with swells created by the storm, splashing up high onto the stone walls. And there he sat, unseen by anyone else, planning how to make things right. Because make things right he would. But he had to take things carefully, think things through first.

There was only one person who he knew had good sense and advice, who was wise and who loved him unconditionally—his brother Zeeshan, King of Ahmar, who had left the castle the night before to return to his palace in the capital city. He'd go there and talk things through. And maybe then he could figure out how to keep Lauren. Because if Lauren believed he'd let her go, she didn't know him at all.

But in the meantime, he had no choice but to stay away from her. Because she was right. He didn't know if he could love. And, until he knew, he needed to keep his distance. He owed her that much.

A DAY later Rayan returned from seeing his brother, Zeeshan. There was something about being with his brother, who knew everything about him, which always settled Rayan. And it had been no different with his last meeting.

It was as if Zeeshan had held up a mirror to Rayan, forcing him to see himself as Zeeshan saw him—someone who'd been cruelly mistreated and had created a barrier between him and the world with which to shield his heart. Zeeshan had challenged him to find the strength to drop the shield and to let love enter his heart and soul. And then he'd said something which puzzled Rayan. He'd told him that loving a woman was the best thing that could happen to him. That it had been the same for him and he'd lost the woman he loved—she'd disappeared out of his life without a trace. Zeeshan had told Rayan not to let the same thing happen to him.

Rayan was shocked. This was the first he'd heard of Zeeshan having loved and lost a woman. But he hadn't been able to probe Zeeshan for any other information. And he hadn't tried too hard. He had his own problems. So he'd left with a new hope in his heart that he could turn things around between him and Lauren.

As if to underline his new sense of hope, the day was clear and bright, and the port buildings and castle were cleanly washed and shining in the sunlight. It was as if the storm had cleared away the old, to make away for a brand new day.

He ran up the steps to the castle, hardly able to contain his impatience to see Lauren again. He went into the drawing room, but it was empty. He was surprised. At that hour she was usually with Salma organizing the day, dealing with any household issues or problems people seemed to bring with increasing frequency to her door. She was a soft touch with them. He smiled at the thought. She was all heart, while he was the opposite, but that was all about to change.

Zeeshan had challenged him to love, and as soon as he'd accepted that challenge he felt like a new man.

He looked outside, but the terrace was empty. Maybe she wasn't feeling so good and was still in bed. He frowned, annoyed with himself that he'd spent the night in the capital city with his brother. He should have returned straight home. He smiled again as he realized he'd named the castle 'home'. He couldn't remember the last time he'd called a place home.

He opened the door, but there was only Salma stripping the bed.

"Where's Lauren?"

Salma's face paled. "She's not here. Didn't you know? I thought she'd told you."

Fear gripped his gut. "Told me what?"

"She's gone."

He swallowed. She wouldn't have gone far. "Gone where? The town? The city? The desert?" He stepped closer to

Salma, who now looked positively scared. "Where, Salma? Where did my wife go?"

She shook her head. "I don't know for sure. One of the admin staff said that she came and used the computer to make some travel arrangements but she deleted the history so we don't know where she's gone."

He strode over to the desk by the window and opened the small drawer where she kept her valuables and paperwork. Her passport was gone.

# CHAPTER 12

*The le Harivel Estate, Norfolk, England*

"Thank God you saw sense and came home, Lauren."

Lauren looked up to her father's still handsome, tanned face. The once chiseled jaw was softened by too much good living, and his blue eyes—the same cornflower blue as her own—were blood-shot from too much alcohol. But he still had the same old aristocratic confidence which beguiled most people—most people, that is, except her anymore.

She opened her mouth to speak, but closed it again with a sigh. What was the point in telling her father that, yes, she had seen sense, but not in the way he imagined?

"Come here, darling. Give your old Dad a big hug."

Her exasperation melted as he folded her into his arms. He'd always been a demonstrative man. She couldn't ever remember a time when he didn't open his arms wide for her to snuggle into. She'd always felt safe there, inhaling the familiar smell of whiskey and tobacco. When he was present, he was very present, but he was away a lot and then—she'd come to realize—he totally forgot about her.

Now, as she pressed her cheek against the scratchy lapel of his tweed jacket, she had to agree with her father's statement—she truly did see sense. Because she saw him for exactly what he was—a charming, feckless man with a warm but shallow heart, more in love with himself than anyone else. She saw him as a whole, complete person for the first time.

Lauren wasn't sure what she'd been hoping for by returning to her family estate in Norfolk and to her father. Reconciliation with her father? A test to see how she felt when she returned to her old home? All she'd known for certain was that she couldn't move on by turning her back on the past; she had to make peace with it.

And she had. It hadn't taken long—only a few days for her to find a clarity of vision which had always eluded her. The estate didn't need her—it was well managed; the old manor house in which she'd been hidden away for most of her life was just that—an old house, not a home; and her father, who she'd thought to be the best man in the world, *wasn't* the best man. He was simply a vain man who lied easily—both to others and to himself. But he was still her father.

"I'm so sorry you had to go through all of this." He glanced down at her swollen belly. "I've made a doctor's appointment for you to get that fixed up—"

She shook her head with slow, clear decisiveness. "I'm not going to any doctor's appointment."

Her father released his hands from her shoulders in a dramatic flourish. "Don't tell me you wish to have the child!"

"I wish to have the child," she repeated calmly.

"Oh, for God's sake!" He tapped his jacket for his cigarettes, and withdrawing one, walked to the library desk and picked up the lighter, waving it as he spoke. "You are a le Harivel, Lauren"—he sparked the lighter, and the flame drew out long and amber in front of his face, creating shadows which aged him—"and don't you forget it!"

She sighed. "I wish I could," she murmured.

"Oh, Lauren! For goodness' sake, now you're talking nonsense!" He strode over to the window and looked out across the park. She came up behind him and looked over his shoulder. Her gaze was automatically drawn to the stables where she'd first seen Rayan, all those months ago. She rubbed her stomach as if to reassure herself that all that had happened was real. Her father noticed and shook his head, his mouth in a tight, disapproving line.

"I'm keeping my baby, Dad. You'll just have to get used to the idea."

He inhaled a long drag on the cigarette, pushed the window open and exhaled out into the cool morning air, before stubbing it out.

"I thought you'd quit smoking."

"So did I," he said with a rueful smile. "Old habits die hard." He heaved a heartfelt sigh. "You'll have to give me time to get used to the idea. About the baby, I mean."

She could hardly believe what she was hearing. "You're okay with the idea?"

"Hardly okay, but"—he pulled her gently into his side—"you're my little girl and I guess it's my grandchild we're talking about."

Tears sprung to her eyes. She had no idea how much she'd wanted her father to accept her baby until now. "It is. And you'll be a terrible grandfather—giving him treats, spoiling him, entertaining him before disappearing again."

He laughed. "It'll be a girl. And of course I'll dote on her. But, you know, I'm beginning to think I might hang around here a bit more now. I know you might not believe me, but this last year has changed me."

"Really?"

"Yes. You see, I really did love Madaniya."

Lauren stared at her father, shocked. "You did?"

"Yes, I did. Hard to believe, isn't it? A serial seducer like me falling in love." His gaze returned to the hazy blue distant hills—hills which she, too, had always liked to gaze at and imagine what lay beyond. His eyes softened visibly at whatever memories filled his mind.

She frowned as she tried to reframe everything she knew. "Not so hard, I guess. The only time I met her, she seemed really lovely—sweet. I remember she had a beautiful smile."

"A beautiful smile and a beautiful soul. Problem was, she also had a troubled soul. She had an upbringing as dysfunctional, no doubt, as your Rayan had. And his brothers."

Lauren's frown deepened. "I remember when she was here that she burst into tears in the middle of dinner and left. And you followed her. I never did understand what that was all about."

"She'd intercepted a text I'd received from an old flame and refused to believe that it was over. She was so jealous. She'd threatened suicide before, and so I ran after her. I was worried she'd do something silly."

"Did she?"

"She was about to. She'd gone to the lake, and I just stopped her in time."

"The lake?" The lake had always been Lauren's place of peace, her place of refuge. It didn't seem possible that it could also be a place for someone to end their life.

"Yes. We left the next day for the Caribbean. I thought she might be happier there. But she wasn't herself. She kept going on about marriage." He shrugged helplessly. "After your mother, I swore I would never marry again. I didn't *want* to marry anyone. I didn't see the *need* to marry." He sighed. "But she did." There was a long pause. "We argued, and I flew to Miami for a few days on business—not pleasure, as the gossips had pleasure in reporting—and it was there that I discovered what she'd done." He chewed his lip. "I hadn't realized she was pregnant. That was revealed in the coroner's report."

"So you weren't to blame."

"Partially maybe. Such things are complicated. But I loved her and I wanted our relationship to work. But, honestly, I think she was beyond understanding that." He shrugged and shot Lauren a brief, tight smile, which showed more hurt than she'd ever seen in his expression before. "I understand her brothers' reaction. It certainly has a primitive flavor, but I *do* understand. Trouble is, my darling, you got caught up in it all. I'm so sorry."

"I'm not. I found something I thought I'd never have." She rolled forward onto her tiptoes and kissed her father on the cheek. "I think I'll go for a walk."

"I'll come with you."

She rested her hand on his arm. "No, I'll go alone. I want to think."

He nodded. "Of course. You're a smart woman, Lauren, and I've underestimated you your whole life, and I deeply regret that. But I know that, whatever decision you make now, it'll be the right one."

As she slipped away, she glanced back to see that his gaze had turned once more to the distant hills.

By the time Lauren reached the shore of the lake, a light rain had begun to fall. She pulled on her jacket and stood under the shelter of one of the beech trees which edged the lake. The leaves were a brilliant orange and curling at the edges.

They wouldn't last any longer than the next wind. But, for now, they gave her the shelter she needed.

Her father's revelation had shocked her. But then, no one was ever two-dimensional—never wholly bad, or wholly good. So why should she expect anything different with her father? He'd just learned to love later in life than most people. Trouble was, his love had turned into a tragedy. For the first time in her life, she felt sorry for him.

She knew he thought she'd returned for good. She turned the idea around in her mind, looking at it from all sides, holding it up like an exhibition piece—her future. And then something settled in her heart and she smiled. This place always seemed to help her see things clearly. She looked across to the place where she'd used to sit with her mother and, for a minute, thought she could see a shadow of a person on the water. But then the rain cloud moved across the lake, leaving only the reflection of the trees. But the feeling in her heart remained. She felt her mother's presence —whether or not it was there. And it helped her now, just as it had always done.

She closed her eyes at the memory of the games they'd played by the lakeside, of how her mother would come running down the path when they were playing hide and seek. She could almost hear her footsteps on the hardened earth of the path. She opened her eyes wide with shock. She *could* hear someone running along the path.

Instinctively she stepped further under the boughs of the beech tree, wondering who on earth it could be. Then the person emerged and she could see exactly who it was.

She clutched her mouth in surprise. What was he doing here? How did he know where to find her?

She watched as he stopped dead in front of the lake and spun around, searching the lakeside and beyond, before dropping to his haunches and gripping his head. She stepped forward, hating to see him hurting so much. She took another step forward and stopped. She'd come here to think things through on her own, but he'd followed. She should be angry, but she wasn't. She only felt a deep sense of relief.

She walked out of the shelter and kept on walking until she stood behind him. She reached out and placed her hand on his head, and he stilled.

"Rayan," she said softly.

A tremor shuddered through his shoulders and he jumped up, looking at her with an agonized expression, and then brought her tight against him, murmuring words in Arabic into her hair, only some of which she understood.

He stepped away, letting his hands slide down her arms until he held her hands tight while he searched her face.

"I couldn't find you."

Suddenly Lauren remembered her father. "Did you see Dad?"

Rayan frowned and shook his head. "I used the back entrance to the house. The housekeeper said you weren't there, so I came here. And when I couldn't find you I thought... I don't know, I just felt overwhelming despair."

She squeezed his hands and smiled, trying to reassure him, trying to wipe the look of utter devastation from his face. "I'm here."

"You are. But that's the problem. I understand why you want to return home."

She smiled as she realized what he was thinking. "It's true, I do."

"But, Lauren, please, you must reconsider. I'm not the same man I was before. I'll be better."

"Better? In what way better?"

"In every way. I'll be whoever you want me to be, so long as you come back to Ahmar with me. I can't have you out of my life, I simply *cannot*."

Delicious butterflies filled her stomach. She could hardly believe he was saying such things. Was she dreaming it? She closed her eyes and opened them again. No, he was still there, the look of desperation still firmly etched in his eyes.

Tears pricked her eyes. She swallowed. "Rayan, I…" she croaked but, feeling tears threaten, stopped mid-sentence.

He shook his head. "No, please God, no, don't say anything. Let me speak. Hear me out. Lauren, you must know that however I began this journey, it all changed when I met you, because I fell in love with you. Nothing I've said or done has been a lie."

She knew he spoke the truth. There had been nothing false about their lovemaking, no misinterpreting the signals for their bodies. They'd been right for each other from the start, and the feelings had only intensified with time.

"The only lie was the one I told myself," Rayan continued.

She frowned and shook her head. "What lie?"

"I told myself that I didn't feel love. It wasn't true. I was too *scared* to love. You showed me that. I know you don't believe you can trust me, but you can. You can trust in my love for you." He took her hand and placed it against his heart. "It's here, beating for you and only you. I promise you I'll spend the rest of my life proving to you that you can trust me. If you let me." He rubbed her hand as if he wanted to imprint it onto his chest. "Please believe me, Lauren. I've changed. I don't know how to show you but I have –"

"I know," she said quietly.

He didn't hear her to begin with and carried on speaking. "I've changed, and I want to show you the changes I've made, not only inside of me, but back at home with my people. I'm not the same man."

She silenced him with a kiss. "I know, I can see it."

"How can you see it?" He sounded almost indignant.

"I can see it in everything you do and say, how you hold yourself, even."

Rayan grunted. "So I'm that easy to see through, am I?"

Lauren grinned. "Don't get grumpy with me, just because I can read you like a book. Although, I have to say that you're a lot better than most books I've read."

"Such high praise," he said, with a wide grin.

She reached up and kissed him gently on the lips. "Take me home, Rayan."

His eyes widened in surprise. "You're going to return to Ahmar with me?"

She laughed. "Yes, of course."

"I thought…" He trailed off, shaking his head. "I thought you'd returned to England for good."

"All I knew was that I had to return to face up to my past and think things through. I've done that. And I want to go home now. To the only place where I can see a future for you, me and our children."

He gently cupped her face. "Oh, Lauren, I've been so stupid. Can you ever forgive me?"

His face went misty through her tears. "Of course I can. But I want you to do something for me."

"Anything."

"I want you to meet my father. You need to talk to him, Rayan. Try to understand what happened. He *did* love Madaniya, you know. While he was with her, there were no other affairs. He told me that, and I believe him. I know when my father lies—he doesn't try hard to hide it. And he was telling me the truth about his relationship with your sister. Gossip columns love to write about him, whether or not it's the truth. And it wasn't the truth that he left Madaniya for other women. I think your sister, wasn't… wasn't…" She trailed off as she tried to figure out how to tell

Rayan that his sister hadn't been mentally or emotionally stable.

"Madaniya wasn't well. I guess we all knew, but didn't want to accept how ill she'd become."

She nodded. "Will you come to the house? Will you meet Dad?"

During the long pause which followed, Lauren held her breath. This final step would be proof that Rayan was no longer driven by anger.

"Yes." He reached out and caressed her neck. "For you I'll do anything."

She exhaled, releasing her last remaining doubts and fears. "Thank you."

Hand-in-hand, they walked back up the path, past the stables, to the manor house to meet the man who watched them from an upstairs window.

# EPILOGUE

*Four months later...*

Rayan cradled his newborn baby girl in his arms and thought he'd never seen anything, or anyone, more beautiful or precious. He stroked Zara's soft blonde hair and marveled at every little thing about her, finishing with her little hands which, the moment she'd nestled into his arms, had relaxed and stretched out.

"She has the tiniest fingers," he said in awe.

"Well, that's good," said Lauren, looking up from her phone before placing it on the beside table. "Because she'd look odd with fingers your size, or mine come to that."

He glanced at Lauren, who looked ridiculously well and healthy after such a long labor. He couldn't figure out why *he* felt so exhausted while she appeared to be positively blooming—her eyes were as bright as her smile. He didn't realize how stressful it was watching someone you love suffer—even if the result of that suffering was something as miraculous as his little girl, Zara.

"Dad said he'll be arriving on tomorrow's flight as planned."

"Good. I've asked Adam to pick him up."

"Adam?" Lauren grimaced. "Do you think he's the right choice?"

"He's *exactly* the right choice. He even asked to go. It seems he has to see your father for himself. He still can't believe that my meeting with him went so well."

"And I can't believe that both your brothers are willing to put the past behind them."

"Hmm," said Rayan. "It seems they are—at least about this."

Lauren was instantly alert, and Rayan knew that he'd regret having let that slip. But there were some secrets—especially those belonging to his brothers—which he'd never betray.

"You mean your brothers have other secrets they're not willing to put behind them?"

He gave a shrug, which he hoped was non-committal.

"So they do!" So much for his hopes. "What are they?"

"My darling, I may not keep my own secrets from you, but that doesn't mean to say I don't keep secrets."

"Secrets belonging to your brothers."

"Exactly."

"And you're not about to share them any time soon."

He gave her a firm, direct glance, which she knew meant she'd never shift him on this one thing. "I'm not about to share them ever." She gave a little pout, which usually meant she got her own way, but still he shook his head.

"So, you really don't keep any secrets from me?"

He smiled. She knew he didn't, but he was in the mood to tease her, just a little. "Maybe."

Her eyes widened. "Really?"

"Yes, really. But I will tell you my secret now if you promise, on your life, never to tell anyone."

She leaned forward expectantly, and his gaze dropped to her partly open mouth.

"I promise," she said.

"Good. Because if it gets out to my people that I am ruled by my wife and my baby girl, my credibility will be shot."

She grinned. "That's a secret I will keep forever."

MUCH LATER, Lauren lay on the couch watching Rayan show off the now sleeping Zara to his two brothers. Not for the first time, she pondered the differences and similarities between the three men.

King Zeeshan was more aloof than either of the others. He stood a little apart, admiring his new niece from a distance. He was also more thoughtful than the others, less impetuous. But she could well believe he kept secrets from the world, and even his brothers.

Then there was Adam. Like her father, Adam was a dedicated lover of women—all women. But, from what Rayan had told her, it seemed he was about to make a big change in his life and accept an arranged marriage. Did *he* have any secrets? She thought it unlikely. But she suspected he also had hidden depths.

Then there was her Rayan. Her heart melted watching him rock Zara to sleep, although she'd been sleeping solidly for the past half hour. He'd come such a long way since their first meeting, when anger had consumed him and revenge had been his only goal. She doubted anyone else would notice any change—unless she or their daughter were present. He was still the same strong, decisive, quiet man he'd always been, quieting people instantly with his direct, intense stare. But with his family he was a different man—a man motivated by love, not anger.

The three sheikhs of Ahmar—so different and yet so close. Two of them with secrets which, it seemed, would be for others to discover…

**The End**

# AFTERWORD

Dear Reader,

At the beginning of the book I wasn't so sure Lauren would be strong enough for Rayan. But she sure showed her strength to the three sheikhs after she discovered what they'd been planning all along! Being a quiet English woman myself, I enjoyed writing that scene!

Anyway, I hoped you enjoyed the book. The other books in this series are:

The Sheikh's Secret Love Child
The Sheikh's Marriage Trap

Feel the need for more sheikhs? If you haven't already, why not check out my **Desert Kings** or **Sheikhs of Havilah** series? They both feature sheikhs who are used to their every command being obeyed, falling in love with strong women with minds of their own. Sparks fly, and their 'happy ever afters' aren't easily achieved, especially when you add a dash of mystery and intrigue...

***Desert Kings***
Wanted: A Wife for the Sheikh
The Sheikh's Bargain Bride
The Sheikh's Lost Lover
Awakened by the Sheikh
Claimed by the Sheikh
Wanted: A Baby by the Sheikh

***The Sheikhs of Havilah***
The Sheikh's Secret Baby
Bought by the Sheikh
The Sheikh's Forbidden Lover
Surrender to the Sheikh

I couldn't resist writing a novella to finish the Sheikhs of Havilah series. ***Taken for the Sheikh's Harem*** is **FREE** to my newsletter subscribers. (Not available for sale or download anywhere else.) Read on to find out more!

*A powerful sheikh, a feminist academic, and a harem...*

*Dr. Ashley Maitland is an academic who is determined to leave her painful past behind her and forge a university career for herself—even if that means she has to write a sensational book about harems.*

*So she travels to the medieval country of Irem which is as mysterious as its king, Sheikh Zyir. But there she discovers that the only way she can complete her research is to join the sheikh's harem!*

To claim your free copy of Taken for the Sheikh's Harem, all you have to do is sign up for my newsletter—either here or on my website.

Happy reading!

Diana

## THE SHEIKH'S SECRET LOVE CHILD

### BOOK 2 OF SECRETS OF THE SHEIKHS— ZEESHAN AND AMANDA

***A desert warrior, a beautiful surfer, a one-night stand which puts them all in danger...***

*Sheikh Zeeshan ibn Mohammed Aziz, King of Ahmar, believed he'd found the woman he wanted to marry when Samantha Cross came sweeping into his life with her devastating beauty and a character to match. But she'd disappeared without trace with equal speed. When he sees her, heavily pregnant, on the internet, he realizes the baby has to be his and is determined to track her down. He knows what growing up without a father did to his half-siblings, and he won't allow that to happen to a child of his.*

*Sexy, freedom-loving Samantha had only accepted the dare on a whim—flirt with the sheikh of Ahmar and earn some cash. It was supposed to have been easy money and a bit of fun. But she had no idea the 'friend' who'd issued the dare was involved with the Russian mafia who planned to lure Zeeshan to his death. As soon as she discovered what was really going on, she went into hiding—away from the mafia who were baying for her blood, and away from Zeeshan, no matter the heartache that would bring. It was too dangerous—for both of them—for her to stay.*

*But she hadn't taken into account the determination of a man scorned, and not just any man—a sheikh, a desert warrior, a man who'd stop at nothing to get what he wanted.*

ALSO BY DIANA FRASER

***Desert Kings***

Wanted: A Wife for the Sheikh

The Sheikh's Bargain Bride

The Sheikh's Lost Lover

Awakened by the Sheikh

Claimed by the Sheikh

Wanted: A Baby by the Sheikh

***The Sheikhs of Havilah***

The Sheikh's Secret Baby

Bought by the Sheikh

The Sheikh's Forbidden Lover

Surrender to the Sheikh

***Secrets of the Sheikhs***

The Sheikh's Revenge by Seduction

The Sheikh's Secret Love Child

The Sheikh's Marriage Trap

***The Mackenzies***

A Place Called Home

The View from Cliff House

Escape to Shelter Springs

What you See in the Stars

Second Chance at Whisper Creek

Summer at the Lakehouse Café

***Lantern Bay***

Yours to Give

Yours to Treasure

Yours to Cherish

Yours to Keep

***Italian Romance***

The Italian's Perfect Lover

Seduced by the Italian

The Passionate Italian

An Accidental Christmas

Printed in Great Britain
by Amazon

79333989R10108